THREE ALIENS WALK INTO A BAR

The Invasion of Lake Peculiar Book 1

JACK RAVENHILL

STERLING & STONE

Chapter One

Journey Devereaux ran through eerie deserted streets. The sound of chanting voices carried on the breeze whipping across a glittering lake up ahead. Dozens of people, maybe more.

She knew she was dreaming because she could see again, but it wasn't regular sight, like before the accident. It was strange. Decentralized, fractured — like she was looking through the eyes of an insect. No, like she was gazing through the eyes of many people at once. Different places and different directions. Somehow her brain was still making sense of it.

And, of course, she knew she was dreaming because it was not just any dream. It was one of *those* dreams. Capital D. She'd been having this one for weeks, night after night, no matter how much she wanted it to stop.

Three times the dreams had come for her, bringing dire warnings. She had acted on them, rescued people. And paid the price.

Now the fourth was hounding her, pulling her along in its undertow.

Journey kept running through streets so empty it seemed like the disaster had already happened. Not like the second dream, with the villagers going about their lives.

Seven people came around the corner, walking in unnatural lockstep. They waved at her and smiled — synchronized, unnatural, freaky.

She didn't wave back, and they didn't seem to mind. As she ran by them, their smiles never flickered.

The chanting grew louder as she got closer.

Journey rounded the corner then skidded to a halt. There, as it had been every night, was the crowd.

A throng of people sitting in concentric circles, cross-legged and swaying.

This should have been in some mountain retreat. They should have been in orange robes or something. If this had been a normal dream, they would have been. But they were regular people, blue-collar folks and soccer moms and grandmas in flowered shirts, sitting on the sprawling lawn, spilling over onto the sidewalk, leaving a little space around the blue park bench and the fire hydrant and the municipal garbage can.

In the center of the crowd stood three gigantic strangers. Each was over seven feet tall and totally bald, with ash-white skin. They stood back to back to back, peering out over the crowd with neutral little smiles. Like angels, or towering muscular pallid Buddhas.

The crowd swayed back and forth, chanting contentedly, and Journey knew — didn't know how, but knew without a doubt — that their selves were being slowly scrubbed away by a strange and distant power that was gaining a foothold in this happy little town she'd never been to.

Beyond the crowd, beyond the strangers, rose a fantastical building. A cathedral of vivid blue glass superimposed on a humble stone church, as if someone had patched and repaired the crumbling stones with unbreakable sapphire, then gone on to spin the crystal into a branching spire with a high, peaked roof and soaring, impossible flying buttresses.

It was the first time a dream had been symbolic, and she had no idea what it meant. The others had been almost shockingly literal. Her dog, Ziti, running out into Elmer Road in front of the yellow house with the patchy brown lawn and getting hit by a red Chevrolet. The shabby tenement next to the 7-Eleven at the edge of the village on the hill that had been the mudslide's first point of impact.

This was completely different. Impossible. Metaphorical. Even in the dream, she felt relief. That meant it couldn't be real, and *that* meant the dream couldn't exact whatever sacrifice it had for her this time. Her stomach tightened in anticipation of the end of the dream.

One of the strangers turned toward her. Unable to resist, she met his gaze.

Her vision went dark. She was as blind in the dream as she was awake.

And she woke up.

"Damn!" Journey sat up in bed and grabbed her drink from the bedside table.

Tears burned their way into her eyes, but she held them at bay fiercely, gulping water then slamming the bottle back down.

But she couldn't hold it off. The dread of a new dream was still in pursuit, nipping at her heels like a horde of shadow wolves. The memory of sight — even the strange, fractured-dream sight — was too painful to let go of, too painful to cling to, too raw in the vulnerable moment after waking.

And that last moment was even more terrifying. It

happened so fast, it would have been easy to overlook. But every night, the dream was the same. She wished she were wrong, but she knew it was true. She wasn't just waking up blind again. She was going blind again in the dream.

It didn't make sense. How could you go blind *again*? But there it was. And not knowing was the greater terror.

The dreams had never told her the sacrifices they would require. They only told her the dangers, the crises she could help avert if she chose to.

She hadn't known what to do about the first dream. She had done nothing, and Ziti had died.

Years later, when the second came to her, she recognized it as the warning it was and prepared. She and her parents had gotten the word out, then they hiked through Quetico Provincial Park to the village on the east face of Gardner Mountain. For three days, they worked with a team of volunteers and first responders, evacuating as many of the villagers as they could manage. A skeleton crew, of course. Not many people were willing to act on the dreams of some girl, and the government's support had been grudging at best. They managed to evacuate almost two hundred people before the mudslide hit. Hundreds of lives saved — almost half the village.

But her parents hadn't made it. They were in the tenement building, trying to convince a few more residents to leave.

And then it was too late.

The third dream had been just over a year ago, and she'd convinced herself that would be the end of it. Tried to, anyway, but...

With great effort, she cut off the litany — a sure path to a depressive tailspin.

Journey lay in bed, doing her best to brush off the

lingering dread the dream always brought. She touched the clock. 5:12 AM.

This one couldn't be real. It had to be some kind of psychological quirk. Her brain had learned that she occasionally had these dreams, and it was simulating the experience. Probably her version of a stress dream. The brain built those out of whatever spare parts it had lying around. She still had dreams where she was back at the deli with sandwich orders piling up, the slicer's blade falling off, some guy trying to crawl over the counter to help, and then she'd realize she was only wearing her apron. It had been a stressful job, and now her brain used facets of it when it needed to run through its paces in the night.

It had to be the same thing with this latest dream. Those freakish, inhuman white men, bald and implacable and a head taller than the surrounding crowd? That wasn't a real thing. Neither was the weird blue crystal that had been interwoven with the crumbling stones of a little church. Nor were the people, who acted like they were in some crappy horror movie or a documentary about a cult.

And yet, as much as she tried to talk herself out of it, she couldn't shake the deep core certainty that it was all just as real as the other dreams had been. There was no way it could be, and yet, it was. It wasn't that she had convinced herself. It wasn't that she believed it was real. It simply *was* real, and she knew it like she knew her house existed. She could try as hard as she wanted to ignore it or talk herself out of it, but reality didn't care what you thought about it. It just was.

And that terrified her.

Journey had cried and cried when the third dream started. The dreams never told her what the price would be, just the doom that was on its way. So she'd been convinced, when the third dream came, that she was going to lose her grandmother, the only family she had left. They'd managed to make some kind of life together after Journey's parents died trying to evacuate people before the mudslide.

She'd raged against the third dream, shrieking in anger as she woke, sobbing at the futility of resisting the inexorable warnings. Night after night, like standing on a train track and watching the locomotive get closer and closer.

Journey had bargained with whatever unseen force was sending the dream. Tried everything she could think of, to no avail. Then it happened. The price came due. But she hadn't lost her grandmother.

She had lost her sight.

Now she lay awake in bed, beyond tears, almost beyond fear, numb with dread and anticipation. What more could the dreams possibly take from her?

Abruptly, Journey got out of bed and began angrily tugging on her clothes. It was far too early to get up, but she couldn't fall back asleep. And her thoughts were terrible company.

She padded downstairs to find the welcoming sizzle and smell of bacon and eggs.

"Grandma? What are you doing up?"

"Sleep is for the uninteresting," said Grandma June briskly. She did almost everything briskly, and she did almost everything. There were forty year olds behind her on the latest tech trends and sixty-five-year-old retirees less active — and she was pushing ninety.

Journey walked over and reached out for a hug. She stepped into her grandmother's embrace and was comforted by her small, bony warmth.

Then Grandma June turned back to the frying pan. "You hear about these spheres?"

Journey's brow furrowed. "What spheres?"

"The Astral App. It caught some blips on a trajectory to earth."

"What do you mean, blips?"

"Objects. A small cluster. Closer than you'd expect, and all headed in the same direction. Their acceleration curves aren't explicable purely in terms of local gravity wells."

"English, Grandma June."

"It looks like they're moving under their own power."

"That's not possible." Journey found a chair and sat. The dread she'd been trying to escape clutched at her again, more forcefully than before. She had found ways to adjust since she'd lost her sight, but now she found herself wishing she could see June's expressions, get any sense of what the old woman felt about this. "Grandma June?"

"It could be fine. Could be a whole new chapter for us." *Us* meant humanity, of course. She had always been a big picture thinker.

"Or it could be the end."

"The end is rarely the end," said Grandma June cryptically. "When you get to be my age, you start to realize that."

"What the hell do you mean, 'the end is rarely the end'? You of all people..." Journey didn't finish the thought. Or have to. She wasn't the only one who'd lost family when her parents died heroically in the mudslide.

"And still, here we are," said Grandma June quietly. "We've both seen a lot of endings, honey."

"This one could be *the* end. Of everything."

"It could. Of humanity, at least. Although we've just learned even that doesn't mean the end of all life."

"I don't care about all life! I care about us. You and me. The park. Our planet. Whatever. It matters if all that goes away. Some endings matter. Even if they're not the end of everything that's ever been."

There was a crack and a sizzle as Grandma June added an egg to the pan. "Let me make you some breakfast, honey. One egg or two?"

"I'm not hungry." Journey walked quickly to the front door. She pulled on her shoes and jacket, grabbed her cane and assist, then stepped out into the cool morning air, ignoring Grandma June's voice calling her back and letting the door slam hard behind her.

It felt good to move, to let out the fears and frustrations that had been brewing within her.

The gravel path crunched underfoot before surrendering to a carpet of pine needles. She folded her cane and paced through the woods, relying on the assist's quiet cues and her familiarity with the terrain to keep from stumbling or walking into a tree.

A background part of her brain worked to track her path, but Journey knew it was futile. The forest was never quite as predictable as the sidewalks and landmarks in town. She'd let the assist direct her back home when she was ready to return. For now, all she wanted was to get away.

Chapter Two

"Road trip!" said Gus. "Come on, start packing your things."

"What?" Sam started awake, already nervous. Not just about Gus. Sam was always nervous. "What do you mean, road trip? What road trip? What things?"

"All the things you'll need. Today we ride. Today we go a-questing." Gus was triumphant, almost majestic. That was probably his theater geek coming through. Sam had always envied the gregarious confidence Gus seemed to have gotten from his time on the stage. Or maybe it was the other way around. All that showy bellowing was a natural fit for the theater. Either way, it beat the hell out of Sam's nervous mumbling and overthinking.

Although, to be fair, overthinking everything did give him access to a wide variety of perspectives he might not otherwise—

Blast.

He was doing it again.

And meanwhile Gus had been going on about something, waxing eloquent like some kind of Roman orator.

"Sorry, what?"

"Knights errant. As. Of. Old. I swear, Sam, you've gotta start listening. You suck the drama out of everything. I'm not gonna stand here rallying the troops and then have someone go 'What?' right in the middle of it. Wrecks the whole rhythm. You know?"

"Yeah. Sorry. So …" Sam stumbled out of bed then began pulling on some clothes, wondering if it would be horribly inappropriate to ask Gus what he had been rallying the troops for. Especially since he was the only troop in sight.

But Gus rolled his eyes and saved him the trouble. That was the great thing about Gus. If you were having trouble contributing to the conversation, you could pause for a second and he would handle the whole thing himself.

"We ride in search of my lady love. The fair, the mellifluous, the radiant NightFoxXx42."

"Oh." Of all the quests Gus might have thought up, this wasn't the one Sam had expected. "We do?"

"We do!" Gus thrust a fist in the air.

Sam continued trying to feel out the situation while doing his best not to suck out all the drama. "So, this is a guild thing."

"Not at all, my bosom companion. This is as AFK as it gets." For a moment he broke character, the grandiose tone falling away. "Why would I tell you to pack all your things if this was in Warduster?"

Warduster, where Gus and Sam spent most of their time outside of work.

"Good point." Sam's brow furrowed. "Wait, why would we go on a road trip to find Night Fox? Didn't you just talk to her?"

"Sam, Sam, Sam."

"Yes?"

10

Gus clapped a hand to his forehead and shook his head in weary disbelief. "Sam, Sam, Sam, Sam."

"That's me."

Gus grabbed him by both shoulders and peered seriously into his eyes. "Sam."

"Still here."

"I worry about you, Sam. I fear for you. I fear that if it were not for my constant watch, you would be dead in a ditch somewhere. Not unhappy, I imagine. The cheeriest little corpse in the vicinity, no doubt. But dead nonetheless."

"Okay?"

"Situational awareness, Sam. Do you know what has happened?"

"Something happened to you? Something bad?"

"Not to me. To the world. To all of us."

"Oh. I don't really follow the news that—"

"We ride, my loyal squire, because the world has changed."

"Changed?"

"Seriously?" The regal demeanor dropped. "You haven't been watching Astral?"

"Well, yeah. I mean, sometimes …"

"And nobody said anything to you?"

"Some people have said some things. About … you know. Various things." Sam wasn't sure yet what Gus was getting at and honestly didn't care. Gus was always going on about some made-up nonsense, and Sam was still groggy from his second near all-nighter in a row at the office.

"Faith and begorrah! You really don't know? The aliens are upon us!"

"What?" Sam groggily yanked on a retro Star Trek T-shirt. "What are you talking about?"

"The end of all things is nigh. Or the beginning. I don't know! Nobody knows. It's a brave new world, and we shall be at its forefront." He grabbed Sam around the shoulders and yanked him into a side hug, spreading a hand before them both as he peered into the future. "The geeks shall inherit the earth, my boy. And what are we?"

"Geeks?"

"The geekiest! All these years we've invested debating zombie preparedness, studying the voyages of the Starship Enterprise, sitting at the feet of the master — Angus MacGyver. All the scenarios we've run in Zarak'Thul. The precision raids we have mounted to glorious victory—"

"None of those are real, Gus."

"Real enough, my boy. While they laughed us to scorn, we were training for this day. While they sat smug in their—"

"Wait, go back. Did you say aliens? Like actual aliens? In real life?" Despite the sleep deprivation, Sam found himself suddenly quite awake.

"Aliens! Well, anomalies, technically. They're too far out for scientists to know anything yet. But it's aliens. You'll see. The news is starting to pick it up. It'll be trending in hours. You're lucky you've got a canny friend like me to interpret the times and the seasons for you, young Sam."

"We're the same age."

"Absolutely. Absolutely. Whatever you have to tell yourself, my young ward."

"What kind of anomalies are we talking? They pick up a green flash or something? Because that's a known—"

"Nothing of the sort. *Objects*. And they seem to be accelerating. I'm telling you, Sam. This is the big one. This is where it all begins."

Sam wasn't so sure. Space was full of objects, many of them accelerating in all sorts of directions for all sorts of reasons. It was probably the gravity well from some undetected mass. Heck, that was how they detected undetected masses in deep space. You found objects getting unexpectedly deflected into a new trajectory. At least, he was pretty sure. He wasn't an astronomer. But still. Gus was always getting excited about one thing or another and then more often than not going off half-cocked on some grandiose project and dragging Sam along in his undertow.

Which was all well and good, at least when it didn't involve tents or homemade crossbows or too much time off work on short notice. Truth be told, Sam kind of liked having someone around to bring ideas to the table keep things interesting.

But he still had to show up for work on Monday.

"So these 'accelerating objects' are aliens why, exactly?"

"Trust me. I've got a good feeling about this. Now quick! There's no time to explain!" Gus broke into a huge grin. "I've always wanted to say that."

"You say that at least twice a week."

"Just like I've always wanted."

Gus grabbed a duffel bag and shoved it into Sam's arms. "Here. I've taken the liberty of packing you a few essentials. Now, come on. Time's a-wasting."

Sam unzipped the duffel and started rooting through it.

"Cereal, Mountain Dew, more cereal. Duct tape. Two tubs of beef jerky?"

"Proper provisions are essential. It's going to be zombie-contingency-mode out there."

"Did you think to bring me, like, a change of clothes or anything? Or toothpaste?"

"Pack your own frivolous luxuries, if you must. We ride within the hour."

With a shake of his head, Sam began stuffing clothes

and necessaries around the tubs of jerky. "And what does this have to do with Night Fox, again?"

"What does this have to do with Night Fox? What does this have to do with Night Fox? What do you mean, what does this have to do with Night Fox?"

What, exactly, could he clarify about a question like that? "What does it, you know, have to do? With Night Fox."

Gus threw up his hands and wandered off into his own bedroom. Sam tried desperately to think of a different way to ask the question. He failed.

"Do you know," grunted Gus from the other room, "what people do when you tell them you have a Canadian girlfriend?"

Sam zipped his duffel then ambled into Gus's bedroom to find him wrestling an old suitcase — his go bag — out of the jammed-together pile that constituted the bottom half of his closet.

"Depends what you tell them about her." Sam had a sinking suspicion he knew the real answer. "Ask if she's hot?"

"They laugh, Sam. In extreme cases, they mock. At minimum, they take it as a rhetorical device. There is no such thing as a Canadian girlfriend, Sam. To these troglodytes, the term is synonymous with a sad lack of game." He rose and shoved the go bag at Sam, who scrambled to rearrange his duffel before Gus let go. "But I've got game, Sam. In spades. So much, it's almost embarrassing."

"Totally!" Sam was a bit overeager, wondering whether that had been a compliment or an insult.

"Walk with me." Gus briskly led the way out the door of their little apartment. "You don't get a girlfriend like Night Fox without mad skills. I'm an alpha in a world of betas, Sam."

"That's why we get invites to all the private" — he caught himself too late then ended awkwardly — "betas."

Gus looked glanced back to make sure he wasn't bing mocked, then gave a small grunt of satisfaction when he saw Sam's face.

"At any rate, Night Fox is not a rhetorical device. She is a living, breathing night elf paladin and my actual girlfriend."

"Totally."

"The fact that she is online and Canadian is immaterial."

"Totally."

"But the impending end of all things has cast our situation in a new light. Time is short, Sam."

"Yeah?"

"Yeah. It's time to prove to the troglodytes once and for all that we're not laughingstocks."

"We're not? I mean, yes!"

"And that is why you and I, my bosom companion, are going on a road trip to Canada to find my lady love Night Fox and seek a token of her l— er, favor."

"What kind of a token?"

"A kiss! A kiss from my lady love before world's end."

"And we're going in your Prius?"

"It's a fine car. It's a great car. Efficient. German." Gus slapped an efficient fist into his palm.

"Japanese," Sam murmured.

Gus was undeterred. "I'd wager there is no better vehicle for an apocalypse."

"Totally." Sam was torn. He hated to ruin the moment but, "It's just—"

Gus's brow furrowed. "What?"

"It's just that I have a really important meeting first thing Monday. So …"

Gus waved this away. "Not a problem. Load the car. Today we ride!"

"Totally. It's just—"

"And be quick about it," Gus added, unlocking his car with a remote chirp. "I'm going to need help carrying our supplies from the shed."

"That's the landlady's shed," Sam called, juggling the bags into Gus's trunk.

"Immaterial!"

Chapter Three

Twenty minutes later, Gus, Sam, and a back seat full of assorted shed paraphernalia were driving at high speed through the heart of Denton, Iowa.

"Gus, we can't just — do that!" insisted Sam as Gus drove dangerously fast down North Street. "Don't you get it? We're felons. We stole those rakes. And the — whatever all that stuff we stole was!"

"Petty criminals, at best," Gus retorted with supreme confidence, before shouting at an elderly woman crossing the street in front of them. "Learn how to drive!"

"But this is horrible! I've never stolen anything before in my life. We're robbers."

"Technically burglars," Gus corrected. "But don't worry your pretty little head about it, my boon companion. This is DEFCON Two. Maybe Three. Martial law applies. Zombie-contingency-mode. And besides, I'm pretty sure the gas can was mine. Get out of the street!" He honked a few times at some pedestrians who looked like they were thinking about crossing.

"There's no way you've ever owned a gas can," Sam protested.

"Immaterial."

"Where are we going?" Sam glanced nervously back at the crowd of angry pedestrians in their wake.

Gus winked and tapped the side of his nose.

Sam wasn't exactly sure what that meant. It seemed like maybe a British thing.

"You leave that to me." He switched to his Blackadder voice. "I 'ave a cunning plan."

"I'm kind of getting a bad vibe." Sam glanced nervously out his windows. Something was off. Denton was usually a quiet, friendly little town. The sort of place where three strangers would say *Good morning* between your house and the coffee shop. But now there was a tension in the air — groups of people clustering on the sidewalks, looking scared or arguing or both. And something else, right at the edge of his consciousness.

And then he placed it. Honking. Sam couldn't remember the last time he'd heard a car honking in downtown Denton, and now he could hear three separate horns.

In the circumstances they sounded scared, surreal, almost creepy.

"God dammit," Gus swore. "The streets are filling up. People must be starting to get the news. We're gonna have to take the back roads."

"Won't that be even worse?"

"No, man." Gus tapped his temple. "Gotta be smart. Do the opposite of your instincts. People are going to go all herd mentality and do the first thing that comes into their heads, and that means everybody tries to get onto North Street to get out of town, which means *we* get off of North Street—"

"And stay in town?" asked Sam.

"No, dum-dum. That makes no sense. You've get the instincts of a suicidal lemming."

"You said we should do the opposite of—"

"Quiet. I'm thinking."

"I thought you said you had a cunning plan."

"I do! That's what I'm thinking about. Hush."

"Maybe—"

"Ssh-ssh-ssh."

"Walmart."

"I said hush!" There was a plaintive note to it, like Gus was mostly annoyed Sam had been the first to say it. Now he'd be stuck arguing against what was the obviously right plan.

Served him right for being a contrarian idiot.

"Walmart is for idiots," Gus said dismissively. "Idiots and lemmings."

"And people who need supplies."

"Lemming-y idiots who find themselves unprepared. That's who needs Walmart. We don't need Walmart. What we need…" Gus pulled off the main drag and began winding through the narrow streets of a residential enclave. The roads curved in lazy traffic-calming sweeps, and it seemed like half were one-ways.

Soon Sam had no idea which direction they were headed. Gus was still driving fast and confident, though, and that gave him some hope. Not a lot, but some.

"A-ha! Perfect." Gus pulled over. His cunning plan, it seemed, was to stop in an isolated cul-de-sac and start rummaging in the back seat.

"You see, young Sam?" he grunted. "Are we unprepared?"

"Yes?"

"No! We have these." Gus proudly raised a pair of sturdy old bow rakes. "And this." Duct tape.

"You're going to … rake the aliens?"

Gus cackled softly and rubbed his hands. "Just you wait. This is going to be magnificent."

Somehow Sam found that more worrying than reassuring.

"Magnificent how, exactly?"

"Never you mind. Just grab these rakes and start hacking their heads off."

That struck Sam as an necessarily gruesome way to put it. "Okay?"

"You got a hatchet, right? Good. Here." Gus thrust a few sticks of jerky at him. "Carb up."

"Those aren't carbs."

"Immaterial. Start hacking."

With a small sigh, Sam started hacking.

IN ONE OF the year-round staff lodgings in Quetico Provincial Park, Ontario, Canada, in a small, wood-paneled upstairs room, NightFoxXx42 was just finishing a raid in Warduster. The workstation was older, but power-ful, and fitted with accommodations for a blind user.

With a magnificent *coup de grace*, she beheaded a final wolfman, mounted her jewel-bedecked white tiger, then rode back to base at a gallop, its huge, soft paws silently swallowing the leagues.

Back at her guild's stockade, she ran a hand along a rack of pigeonholes until she found the one assigned to her. There was a scroll inside. She opened it, and an audio message from Gustavius boomed out in the knightly voice he had chosen for his avatar.

"Night Fox, my lady. The end of all things is upon us." Here the grandiose delivery broke for a moment, the synthetic voice rich and hesitant. "But, like, IRL. I mean"

— the theatrical delivery resumed — "beings from another world have been sighted, wending their way swiftly toward us. And so, I embark on a journey. I come to seek a favor from you, my lady. I ask but a token of your favor, a kiss from your ruby lips before the end of all things. I shall arrive at your doorstep in—" Again the booming voice faltered into a distinctly non-knightly hesitation. "Well, actually, I don't know exactly how long it'll take. I'm guessing things might get a little crazy out there. But I'm on my way. Few days, maybe? Tops. Hopefully sooner. Anyway. You. Me. Ruby lips. Can't wait."

The scroll snapped shut.

Night Fox groaned.

"Well, bugger. That's going to be an issue."

She took off her helmet and gloves then tossed them onto the desk, preoccupied with the new problem.

Downstairs, the door slammed. The kitchen floorboards creaked as someone walked in.

"Grandma June?" called Journey. "Are you home?"

"Yeah, baby," her grandmother answered. "I'm home."

Chapter Four

"Perfect," cackled Gus, rubbing his hands together. "Perfect! No, not like that."

Sam was on his knees in front of the car, tentatively positioning a rake head and wrestling with a roll of duct tape. "Are you sure this is a top priority right now?"

"Of course! This is straight out of Mad Max. Total zombie preparedness."

Sam adjusted his grip on the crudely hacked-off rake head and kept struggling with the duct tape.

"Car spikes might not be the most effective use of our time. I mean, they'll look cool, don't get me wrong, but are they really practical? Especially when it's just, you know …" He limply waved the severed rake head.

Gus growled in frustration.

"Not if you do it wrong. Obviously." He growled again. "Here. Just let me."

Grunting with effort, he got down on his hands and knees then yanked the tape out of Sam's hands. "Just hold it in place."

With a small sigh, Sam took the rake head and did his best to line it head up along the front bumper in a balanced and aesthetically effective manner, the tines of the rake curving up below the driver-side headlight. He tried not to see them as misplaced eyelashes. The effect was supposed to be menacing, not cute. Not that it was really either.

Gus yanked off a few lengths of duct tape, hastily slapped them onto the rake head, then went over it again with several more strips.

"There. See? Easy."

"Well, yeah. I was holding it in place. If you'd been helping me I could have—"

"Immaterial. We'll be unstoppable on the mean streets. This will give us the edge we need as the world devolves into chaos."

Sam started lining up the second rake head. Gus, apparently taking this as a sign that his services were no longer needed, rose then started rooting through their supplies.

"Actually, about that," said Sam. "Do you think we should head back to the apartment first? It's kind of sounding like we're gonna be gone longer than a—"

Gus emerged with a fistful of jerky.

"Sam, Sam, Sam." He shook his head. "Sam, Sam, Sam, Sam, Sam."

Stop saying Sam! He couldn't get it out.

Gus bit off a mouthful of jerky and kept talking around it. "Have you learned nothing? Has my tutelage meant so little to you? We're not lemmings. We're explorers. We don't go back. We go forward. We go onward, to adventure and the grand horizon."

"I mean, that all sounds great, obviously, like, on paper.

And we should totally do it. But I really think we might want to go back and get a little more properly—"

"Let me tell you something, Sam." Gus leaned casually against the car, talking and chewing. "Have you ever heard the story of the little boy who said go back?"

Sam felt a sinking feeling. "Is this a story you're making up on the spot?"

"There was once a little village, and in the village there was a brave knight, and the knight was going to go on a brave journey, to adventure and the grand horizon. But there was a little boy with the knight, and do you know what the boy said to the knight?"

"I'm guessing he said to go—"

"He said go back! But the knight refused. The knight went on to gold and glory, and he became famous and powerful and well-liked. But the boy, do you know what the boy did, Sam?"

"He went back?" said Sam dismally.

"He went back. And do you know what happened to that boy?"

"I'm assuming something b—"

"Wolves, Sam. Wolves happened to the boy. And that's why we don't go back. We go forth." Gus gestured majestically with his fistful of jerky, then yanked off another bite. "Do you want to get ripped limb from limb, Sam? Do you want to stare into the maw of the angry beasts already ravening at our erstwhile door?"

"I don't think there are actually any wolves."

"Immaterial!"

"It's not immaterial!" Sam felt his face growing hot. "I left a ton of stuff back there because I thought we were just going for the weekend. Maybe a few days, tops. If we're really hitting the open road, never to return, with aliens and chaos and the breakdown of society on its way, then we should go back and get the rest of our stuff."

"Look, Sam. I'm not gonna lie. I like where your head's at. Makes a lot of sense on paper. You're a good kid, and I don't want you to think otherwise. But trust me. Right now, going back to our apartment is the last thing we want to do."

"Really? It's kind of the first thing I want to…" He drifted off, trying to ease a tangle out of the duct tape while holding the second rake head in place with one hand.

"You're thinking rationally, Sam. That's the last thing you want to do right now."

"Is it? Because I thought … you know. I would've thought thinking rationally was …" Sam paused, expecting Gus to cut him off as usual.

But Gus just looked at him expectantly.

He wasn't used to having to actually finish his thoughts around Gus. "Um …" he faltered again, still fumbling the second set of spikes into place. "I mean. You know. I would've thought we'd want to think rationally. Usually. Don't we?"

"Do you think the mobs of looters already sweeping our streets are thinking rationally?"

"Not really."

At last he managed to get the second rake head in place. He added a few extra pieces of tape just for good measure then stepped back to look it over.

"Exactly!" crowed Gus. "And look at them, rich with supplies, first to the prime looting zones."

A surge of anger burst up inside Sam. He almost shouted at Gus, finally, for once. Almost.

An impotent, frustrated rage overtook him. He could see all the arguments like they were laid out in front of him. All the mistakes Gus had made, all the contradictory things he'd said to cover his own asinine failures. All the good reasons to go back. The contrarian resistance to a perfectly good plan just because it wasn't his. All of the nonsense counter-arguments. All of the … Gusness.

Sam could see it all. But he couldn't say a thing.

Normally it didn't matter. Normally it was funny. Normally they were just fighting about which superhero would win if you gave them sharks for fists and put them under water or some nonsense that was just fun to get mad about. But this actually mattered. This was—

"Life and death" was the figure of speech that most naturally came to mind, and it brought Sam up short. It wasn't just an expression. He'd never been in a life-and-death situation before.

This time, Gus wasn't just wrong. He wasn't just being an idiot.

This time, Gus could get them killed.

But still the words didn't come out. Some block in his belly, some tightness in his throat held them in.

Instead, he stared impotently at the rake heads messily taped to the front of the car as Gus rambled on about whatever idiot stream of consciousness currently had him in its undertow.

"We're dead," he muttered.

"What? Hogwash! We're alive. We've never been *more* alive!"

"I guess," Sam said doubtfully. "Look, are you sure you don't want to just try to get into a Walmart? I really feel like we could use some better equipment."

"What better equipment? You've got your hatchet, right? We've got jerky. We got a gas can and …" He waved a vague hand at the back seat. "All that stuff. We'll be fine. We're solid. Trust me. The place is getting mobbed. And anyway, we don't want to mess with that mob of plebes."

"Because they'd trample us?"

"No! The opposite of that. We can handle ourselves, Sam. Don't you worry your pretty head about that. Not at all. The reason we don't care to tangle with a Walmart is because it's beneath us. Look at us, Sam. Are we Walmart people? Are we the kind of people who immediately revert to type and go to scramble and scrounge through a big box store with the rest of the rabble at the earliest hint of danger?"

"Yeah?"

"Of course not! We're the originals, Sam. We're the explorers. We're going to find a brand new horizon and loot it like it's never been looted before."

"I don't think you can loot a horizon. And Walmart has—"

"I don't care what Walmart has. I care what we have, Sam. What we have right here." He clapped a fist to his heart. "And in here." He tapped his temple. "And back there." He jerked a thumb at the back seat. "I'm telling you, Sam. We've got protein and we've got sharp objects. We're golden. All we have to do is get out ahead of the crowd and make for the open country."

"No!" The word burst out of Sam before he knew what he was doing.

"What?"

"No. Look." Now Sam's mouth had committed him, and he scrambled to catch up. "You're always plowing through everybody, doing whatever you want, and you act like you're always obviously right and nobody else knows anything, and — and it's got to stop. Okay? We're supposed to be ..." Something in him shut down hard. Whatever he'd been about to say was too dangerous.

"Wingmen."

"Yeah." He felt a strange rush of relief. Wingmen was safe. "And … and we're not. Wingmen stand by each other. And try each other's ideas. And listen to each other."

Actually, he wasn't sure that was really what wingmen did at all, but that wasn't the point. Sam swallowed nervously and waited to see what would happen next.

Gus was giving him a curious look.

"Okay," he said presently.

"Okay?"

"Okay."

"What do you mean, Okay? Okay, what?"

"Okay, let's check out the Walmart."

"Really?"

"Sure." Gus had suddenly gone strangely cold. "Hop in."

GUS STOPPED near the far edge of the Walmart parking lot. The entrance looked like Black Friday, except nobody had bothered parking in the marked spaces. A huge cluster of cars was crammed together around the front door, with everyone honking and yelling at everyone else. A mob of desperate looters climbed over hoods and shoved and punched their way to the doors.

It was the first moment, in all the alien-invasion hubbub, Sam really felt scared. He would remember that sensation long afterward, the sinking dread of seeing the usually-friendly small town of Denton going feral.

And nothing had even happened yet. That was the craziest part. Part of him wanted to shout everyone down, tell them that for all they knew it was just some little bug or anomaly in the app, some dust on the lens of that massive scope on the far side of the moon. How could people this thoroughly lose their minds over a few tiny dots so far from anything?

And yet, of course they were. The only reason Sam hadn't gone full panic-mode himself was because he had a whole lifetime of practice suppressing strong emotions.

Gus hadn't spoken a word since they'd left the cul-de-sac, and Sam sat tensely in the silence. He had gotten his way for once, and it was horrible. His hand ran absent-mindedly along the hatchet he had stolen — kind of stolen — feeling its weight and heft and solidity. It was strong, heavy, reassuring. Almost intimidating. He didn't quite feel worthy of it. It was the kind of tool made for someone who knew what they were doing. Get Sam behind a data pad and he was unstoppable, but when it came to using his actual hands and arms and legs, things got a lot dicier.

And add sharp metal objects and you started playing pretty long odds.

Ahead of them, the mob kept seething at the Walmart entrance.

Sam swallowed. He'd never seen people acting like that. They seemed inhuman, some kind of strange swarm. His hand tightened on the reassuring hardness of the hatchet.

"Okay?" Gus said, out of nowhere.

"What?"

"Are you satisfied?"

Sam could hear Gus's voice turning sour, and his stomach tightened. He'd seen this before. Gus was the sort of person who bottled things up, and then, every so often, the bottle cracked.

"Do you get it now?" Gus asked, a strange tension pulsing in his voice.

Sam didn't answer. He thought he did get it, at some level, but he couldn't put words to it yet. He couldn't make himself look at Gus. Everything in him was tightening up, shutting down, trying to become smaller. Disappear until the storm passed.

"See?" Gus sounded frenetic, almost on the edge of tears. He slammed the steering wheel. "This is what I've been trying — Gah! Don't you see it? You never get this stuff. You just ride along, all la-de-da, and I'm the one who has to—" His voice choked off. "You know?"

"Yeah." Sam didn't know what he was agreeing with. He just wanted it to be done.

"This is why I was saying—" Gus's sentence choked off again. Sam wasn't the only one who'd trained himself to avoid this stuff. "Okay? We're not ... We can't ..."

And then Sam knew what it was that Gus knew but couldn't say. He was terrified. They both were, and it was right that they were, because that was about right since they didn't have a clue. Gus had, in his way, been trying to protect them. Not from the mob, exactly, but from having to face the mob.

And Sam had rubbed his face in it.

"We should go," Sam said.

"No shit, Sherlock," spat Gus. His hands tensed and writhed on the steering wheel. "That's what I was saying."

"Gus, they're just lemmings. Lemming-y idiots. Right? They're nothing." Sam desperately hoped the callback would pull Gus out of it. These moods either flashed and died on the spot or they lingered for days, sometimes weeks. If this one stuck around, it was going to be a rough road trip.

"Yeah. Yeah. Lemmings." Gus was warming, and Sam felt a glimmer of hope.

"You were right. About Walmart. And all of ... That would have been a bad plan." Sam found he couldn't stop himself from babbling, filling space. "If we'd done it, I mean. Tried to go in there for supplies and … you know. We would have had to fight off—"

"Sam, please." Gus raised an authoritative hand, and Sam could hear in his voice that they were out of the woods. "Sam, Sam, Sam. You have much to learn of the ways of the world."

"Totally," said Sam, flooded with relief.

Chapter Five

An hour and a half later, they were thirty minutes outside Denton. Sam was still feeling a little quivery. Gus seemed like he'd gotten past the mood, but he still wasn't talking much. Sam tried to convince himself it was because driving in pre-apocalyptic conditions required extra concentration.

"This Night Fox thing," he said tentatively. "Going to be kind of a three musketeers situation once we get there, isn't it?"

"Two musketeers," Gus said, sounding distracted.

"I just mean … you know. Once you you're actually there with your girlfriend, and I'm there…"

"I don't know what to tell you, man," said Gus. "If you had a girlfriend, maybe we could go find her."

"Yeah," Sam answered miserably.

"Don't worry, man. We'll find you some action, too. Right? Hey, I bet once we've got Night Fox with us, it'll be that much easier to pick up a hot chick in a bar. It's social proof. They'll know we aren't creeps and stuff because she'll already be with us."

"Yeah," said Sam little more hopefully. He'd never picked anybody up in a bar. He hadn't even been to many bars. It wasn't really his scene. Too loud and … jock-y. "You go to a lot of bars?" he asked, even though he knew Gus didn't. Conventions, yes. Gaming meet-ups, check. Comic book stores, you got it. But bars?

"Oh, I think I know a thing or two about the bar scene," said Gus with a confident little smirk.

Sam relaxed a little inside. Not all the way, but a little. "Just one or two things? Because you know, that's not really very many." Now it was Sam's turn to smirk.

"It's an expression!" blustered Gus. "I know plenty. Just you wait and see. I'll pick up Night Fox, then we'll take her out, show her a good time, and you know, with the chemistry the two of us have. we'll be, like, a power wingman. Like, you won't even have a chance."

"That makes it sound like a bad thing."

"No, no. You won't have a chance of *not* getting some action. We're going to be in make-out city, my friend."

"Yeah." Sam felt his excitement rising. Of course Gus wouldn't leave him hanging. I mean, maybe right at the beginning. There was a chance. Like when they first met Night Fox in person. He'd probably want to give them a little space or whatever.

But then, make-out city.

They passed a three-car pile-up on the side of the road, then the traffic started to break up. Gus accelerated.

Sam peered back at the accident. There was a man sitting by one of the cars with a bloody forehead, sobbing. A sick sense of dread crept into his belly.

"Ah, the open road," Gus beamed. "This is freedom, my friend. This is America. This is the *grand dame* herself."

"Totally," said Sam.

Gus glanced over.

"Look, I know what you're thinking. But we'll get you one. Or ... you know. If we don't, you're still ... you know. Your value isn't in the hotness of your girlfriend but in the cut of your jib, and all of that. You're made of stars, Sam. All of that kind of thing. You know?"

Sam felt sick. Suddenly, the whole girlfriend issue felt jarring, irrelevant. Gus's empty words were crowding him. A panicked claustrophobia started rising up in him, choking off his breath.

"It's okay," he managed. "You don't" — he took a quick gasp, feeling short of breath — "have to, you know, keep saying all that stuff."

"Absolutely, absolutely," gushed Gus. "A little peace and quiet would be just the thing right now. Just what I was thinking myself."

He looked over, and Sam was startled to see a touch of nervousness in his eyes. Maybe he wasn't the only one who'd been shaken by how the Walmart Incident went down.

"We should have gone back." Sam rolled down his window and took in a lungful of warm, exhaust-choked air. Far behind them, someone was honking without letting up.

Gus kept his eyes on the road, and for ten seconds or so, silence reigned supreme.

"It wouldn't have been a good idea," Gus said abruptly. "Trust me. The town was already starting to fall apart. It would've been a bad scene."

"Sure."

They would have had time. People were getting antsy, but it wasn't like it had evolved into frontier justice city-states over the course of a couple hours. They could've gone back.

"Look, I told you—" Gus's hands tightened on the wheel, then he balled up a fist and bounced it on his leg.

But it was a small, tight gesture, more of a holding back than a letting go.

"Yeah, no. I know." Sam didn't know what he meant, really. He didn't agree, and for once, it actually mattered. But they were on the knife-edge, and he didn't want to push Gus over.

Gus took a tight breath, his hands still twisting white-knuckled on the steering wheel. Then he relaxed and reached for the audio controls. "Here, listen to this."

Of course he couldn't stand more than ten seconds of silence.

"This guy is kind of amazing." Gus flipped on a cast midway.

"— Templars had about four centuries ago. But you know who the modern-day descendants of the Templars are, right? I'll tell you. And most people — even the people who are paying attention — don't get this right, because they've split into three separate arms. But it's the Rothschild triumvirate — who have a big say in controlling what goes into the mainstream media, by the way — the Ordo Templis Orientalis, and the Dominicans. Or rather, I should say the Vatican Enclave, which is currently being controlled by the Dominicans.

"And you might be asking, 'What are the Templars doing in North America?' Well, that's just it. What was the Templars' original mission back when they were founded? To protect the pilgrimage to Jerusalem. And you can look that up. People don't understand that was only symbolic. It was never about Jerusalem the *city*. Some of you out there know what I'm talking about.

"Now this is an organization that rose to incredible power very quickly — *carte blanche* to operate above the law, even across national borders, whatever they wanted — and what were they doing with it? What *are* they doing with it?

We'll get to that in a second, and I'm not going to lie, it's pretty shocking. But first, I want to take a minute here to tell you about our sponsor, Primal Power Masculine Nutrition Bricks—"

"Do we really have to—" Sam glanced over at Gus. "I mean. It's fine. But this really isn't, you know. My thing. And if we're going to be driving for a long time …" He found himself desperately reading Gus's face for any clue. The last thing he wanted was to invite another sour mood. But the second-to-last thing he wanted was to spend ten hours in the car listening to some kook rant about how the Templars were turning the frogs Catholic. "You know what? It's okay. I'll just listen to my own playlist." He started rummaging for his earbuds.

Gus reached over and flipped off the cast.

"It's fine. If you don't get it, you don't get it."

"Cool," said Sam. "Cool. Totally. Um—"

"I mean, it kind of betrays a certain lack of imagination on your part. Lack of vision, you know. Openness to other worldviews and whatever. But really, that's your call. You can look a gift horse in the mouth, but you can't make him drink. You know?"

"Totally." Sam swallowed. "Um. I mean, we can turn it on for a while if you—"

"No, no. Don't coddle me, Sam. The moment is past. We shall talk of other things."

"Where do you even find this stuff? It's like those crappy B movies you're always watching."

"Pshaw. You know those are the best movies out there. That's what true art is, my friend. You don't know what you're talking about."

"Yeah," Sam muttered. He went back to rummaging for his earbuds.

Gus pressed on. "*Slime Mummies from the Nth Dimension* is

as good as any classic film out there. Fight me. I'm serious. You just don't get that kind of creativity from the regular mainstream media." His eyes widened in a stricken look. "Oh, damn. I'm starting to sound like him."

"Who?"

"Ronan Keats. The guy. From the thing." Gus pointed at the audio controls. "He's, like, a big time conspiracy junkie. And he's better than most of them," he added defensively.

"I didn't say anything," said Sam.

"Yeah, but you were thinking it."

"Well, yeah. Obviously."

"I'm telling you. He's got a cool spin on it. I mean, totally cuckoo balls, of course. But at least he's cuckoo balls in interesting ways. And he's not mean about it. I don't know. I just kind of like the way he presents it, even though you know none of it makes any real sense."

The silence threatened to loom.

"He's local, you know," added Gus, as if everything hung on getting Sam to like this guy. "I think he's actually from a couple towns over from us. Marshall, I think." Gus threw a nervous look his way.

Sam took pity on him. "I tell you what, you can make it up to me. Next time we get to a spot that's got supplies and isn't being mobbed, you're buying me a go bag and everything that goes in it."

Gus beamed. "Hell, yes!"

"And no more idiotic stories about kids getting eaten by wolves that you make up on the spot."

Gus's expression soured. "It wasn't idiotic. It was trenchant, timely. It was a compelling fable of the —"

BANG! BANG!

There was a sudden pair of explosions and the car begin to veer wildly out of control.

37

"Whoa!" cried Sam.

Gus started screaming.

The safety protocols kicked in within seconds, but Gus was still wailing like a little girl.

"Flat tire," the car notified them. "Please deploy spare."

Screaming, Gus braked wildly. They fishtailed to a stop on the side of the road. Other cars flew past, honking their rage as they narrowly avoided a pileup.

"What happened? Gus, shut up. We're fine."

Gus's howl petered out. He took a deep breath.

"Don't start again!" Sam cried. "Just stop for a second. What happened?"

"I don't know!" panted Gus. "It must have been the aliens. Maybe they've got heat rays. Like in War of the Worlds. You know? Like, from a distance."

"There are no aliens, Gus. Not yet, anyway. Car, shut up," Sam added since the car was still repeatedly advising them to deploy the spare.

He opened his door and stepped out onto the hot asphalt. It felt strange and disorienting to be standing on the highway, like you could get run over by a speeding car at any moment, even though he knew that was an irrational fear. Still, he walked around the front of the car instead of the back, leaning gingerly to peer around the corner without getting too near the highway.

Except it didn't take much looking to see what had happened.

"Dammit, Gus."

Both driver side tires were shredded, and the rake they had duct taped under the left headlight was missing.

Gus opened his door a sliver and peeked out. "What happened?"

"The spikes fell off. Tore up both tires."

"Is it bad?"

Sam sighed. "We'll need to put on the spare. I guess we'll have to figure out which one is more strategic to replace. Is your car rear wheel or four wheel drive?"

"Yes! Definitely. I mean, probably. Right? I mean, it would have to be, right?"

Sam rolled his eyes. Gus clambered out of the car and began examining the front driver side wheel. What was left of it.

"Dammit, Gus. Why did we even put these on? Like, even if we were going to ram another car, what were these going to do? Take out the tail lights?"

"No, man. The spikes were just what we needed. Show we mean business. Dominate the roads. You know? Zombie contingency?"

Sam sighed. "What are we going to do, Gus? This is actually bad. Like, I don't think we can drive any more like this. What are we supposed to do? Just … walk until we get to an exit?"

"I guess. I mean, we can't push the car. Can we? Seems like it would be too far."

"We're not going to push the car. I don't know. Maybe we can put on the spare and limp to a rest stop or something. Do you know how to put on a spare?"

"Yeah. I mean, just Google it. Right? Where do you get a spare?"

"I think there should be one. Maybe in the back?"

"At least we've got a hatchet. And some rake poles. That should help. Right? See? Zombie preparedness for the win!"

"I don't think you use rake poles to fix a spare tire," Sam said dubiously. "I mean, that's not, like, a tool people usually have around."

"No, like, you know. To prop up the car or whatever."

Sam looked at the tangle of bags and hardware and loose jerky dominating the back half of the car. It was an avalanche waiting to happen. A sense of weariness settled over him.

"Maybe we can just drive it really slowly. Kind of get to somewhere with a little civilization and then figure out what to do next."

"Can you do that?" asked Gus. "I thought it was bad for it — you know, to keep driving on a flat tire. Or something."

"I mean, yeah, probably. But we've only got one spare anyway. If we even have a spare. Do you really want to dig through all that junk and see if there's one under the seat or whatever?"

"I think it would be in the trunk."

"Sure. Fine. Same question."

"Good point. And it's like you said. We're going to have to drive on at least one of them like this anyway."

"Okay."

"Okay."

"You want to drive or should I?"

Gus just peered at him for a long moment with wide, traumatized eyes.

"Fine," sighed Sam. "Get in the other side."

Gus clambered into the passenger seat and Sam took the wheel.

"Hey, car," snapped Gus. "Where's the nearest mechanic?"

"There's a good one 34.2 miles from here," it pleasantly replied. "Would you like me to give them a call?"

"No."

"Okay. There are a few other options within fifty miles. If you're interested I can—"

"No! Cancel. Forget it." Gus growled. "Curses! That's way too far."

"Car, are there any gas stations or rest stops or whatever nearby?"

"Sure. There's a Whatever-U-Need 4.3 miles from here off the next exit. Looks like they get good reviews. Would you like directions to that one?"

"What's a Whatever-U-Need?"

"It looks like there's one 4.3 miles from here. They get good reviews. Would you like directions to that one?"

Gus snickered, and Sam shot him a look. "Fine. Whatever."

The car switched its nav to the Whatever-U-Need — whatever that was — and Sam shifted into drive.

"I'm sorry," said the car. "It looks like you've got two flat tires. It is not safe to drive. Would you like me to call assistance?"

"Override," snapped Sam.

"Are you sure? This is an important warning. It is not safe to drive the car in its current condition."

"I know. Override. Override."

"All right. I have disabled the safety lockout. Drive carefully, and have a nice day."

"Thanks," muttered Sam.

He turned on the flashers and began crawling the car along the shoulder.

Chapter Six

"This is the worst," moaned Gus. "You can't impress the ladies with a car that's only got two tires."

"Maybe what impresses the ladies is different in Canada. You know, like a hemisphere thing. Like water going down the drain a different way."

"Really?" Gus brightened.

"No."

"Maybe if I just make sure she only gets in on the passenger side …" mused Gus.

Sam remained silent. It didn't exactly take a lot of focus driving down the shoulder at 6.3 mph, but it was the kind of thing you could pretend took a lot of focus, and he was in no mood to deal with Gus right now.

"I'm just saying, it seems like kind of a waste if we get all the way to Canada and then I can't impress her with my sweet ride."

"We don't have to make it to Canada. We just have to get to Whatever-U-Need. I wonder if they have tires."

"Well, do we need them?"

Sam refused to set him up for the obvious joke. Instead he kept his eyes on the road, ignoring Gus for all he was worth.

"Then I guess they'll be at Whatever-U-Need." Gus slid right by the fact that Sam had said nothing and his line was a non-sequitur.

Sam doubled down on the ignoring.

Part of him wanted to tell Gus, *You know, you're not the only one who wants a girlfriend here.* To which Gus would insist that he didn't *want* a girlfriend, he *had* a girlfriend. And Sam wouldn't bother correcting him because it would just make Gus sad, which would make him act mad and get all defensive and insist that an online Canadian girlfriend you'd only ever seen as an in-game avatar totally still counts.

And fine, say it did count. If anything, that reflected even worse on Sam's current situation. What kind of loser couldn't even manage to get himself a virtual girlfriend? And goodness knows he spent enough time playing Warduster.

He knew what the problem was, of course. He needed to learn to speak up, stand up for himself, make his voice heard. Turned out it greatly reduced your chances of getting a girl to go out with you if you never asked her out.

Still, part of him couldn't help blaming Gus for always hogging the spotlight, always making it about himself. The road trip was a perfect example. Sam's excessively reasonable mind wouldn't let him fault Gus for hauling him along. Sam was always up for an adventure, and most of them were Gus-centric. But it would've been nice to have some chance at his own romantic end-of-the-world quest. Past a certain point, it got old being a spectator to somebody else's life.

And that raised another, even darker angle. What would happen to Sam once Gus and Night Fox were actually together in real life? He was happy for Gus and all, but there was no way things were going to be the same once he had a hot girl on his arm.

"In fact," Gus said, "if it's really a Whatever-U-Need, you know what they might have for you?"

Sam kept his eyes on the road, getting ready to not acknowledge the inevitable answer. *A girlfriend.*

"Some taste in movies."

"Shut up, Gus."

At long last, the Whatever-U-Need came into sight. Or rather, the building finally did. The sign out front was elevated far over the highway in garish red and yellow. Sam had spotted it halfway down the exit.

He limped into the parking lot.

"Pull up to the pumps. Let's get some gas," said Gus.

"Shouldn't we make sure we can get it into drivable shape again before we waste money on gas?"

"Sam, Sam, Sam," Gus retorted, shaking his head. "There is no such thing as wasting money on gas in a scenario like this. If worst comes to worst, we can cut out the gas tank and carry it with us as a post-apocalyptic currency. Fuel is king."

"We're not gonna cut a gas tank out of—" Sam was incredulous. "You don't even know how to change a freaking tire."

"Immaterial. Pull up to the thing."

"Fine. But you're paying."

Gus stared him down. Sam, for once, didn't back down.

"Fine," snapped Gus. He indicated one of the pumps. "Pull up to the thing."

Sam rolled the car a final few feet and, after a brief slap fight, successfully made Gus get out to pump the fuel.

Sam, meanwhile wandered into the Whatever-U-Need to look for a miracle.

Chapter Seven

There was a knock at the door.

"Are you expecting anyone?" Journey asked.

"No." Grandma June sounded puzzled.

Journey heard her starting to get up and waved her down. "I'll get it."

This was one of the parts about being blind that she especially hated. Maybe it was different for people who'd been born to it, but meeting strangers without being able to look them over still felt like diving feet first off an unknown edge. Still, it wasn't going to get any better, and she preferred to practice the hard moment rather than practicing avoiding it.

She opened the door a crack, throttling thoughts that were already swirling with a dozen different scenarios. An armed burglar. A handsome stranger. A crowd of looters getting away from the aliens. For all she knew she was staring down a shotgun. At least if she died, she'd go down looking brave. "Yes?"

"Ma'am?" said a polite young male voice. "I'm with Parks Canada. I'm sorry to tell you we're evacuating the staff settlement. The parks will be closed to the public effective tomorrow morning at eight. Staff will have forty-eight hours from then to make any necessary arrangements and evacuate the premises. Emergency accommodations will be provided if you need them."

"What?" cried Journey, even as June came up behind her with an angry, "Just a minute, now."

"This precaution is being taken for the sake of public safety," the young man said. Journey wondered how many times he'd had to get through this spiel already today, how many times he'd been yelled at or cried at. Or punched.

"The hell it is!" snapped Grandma June. "How the hell are we supposed to get out of here in two days? What are we going to do? She's blind. I'm eighty-eight. What, are we supposed to mosey out to our summer house in Bermuda for a few weeks until this all blows over?"

"Emergency accommodations will be provided if necessary," he repeated. "In cases of undue hardship, please notify Parks Canada Agency of your particular circumstances. We will strive to accommodate you to the best of our ability."

"Look at me," commanded June. "Look at my eyes. You're gonna give me the brush-off and what, we'll sit on hold with them for a few hours and then wash, rinse, and repeat until it's time to leave?"

"I'm sorry, ma'am, but I don't have a lot of time to discuss it. We're working to notify every household within the park borders in a very limited timeframe."

"Why are they doing it?" asked Journey.

"It's for the public safety. In the wake of the recent anomalies sighted on the Astral App—"

"Oh, who are you kidding? Just call them aliens," snapped June.

"—a large number of individuals have attempted to seek

refuge within park territory. Many of them are ill-equipped, and the Agency is not prepared to monitor and protect them at this volume. The decision was made early this morning to shut down public access to the parks for the time being in the interests of public safety. The emergency shutdown will go into effect at eight a.m. tomorrow, with the staff evacuation deadline forty-eight hours later. The marshals' service will be on hand to assist any residential staff remaining at that point with evacuation. Any residents who fail to comply may be prosecuted under Section 204.8 of the Operations Code."

There was a pause, and Journey could practically see Grandma June's steely glare.

"I really am sorry," said the young man after a moment. "There's nothing I can do about it. Stay safe."

Journey heard him start to walk away.

"Come back here!" shouted Grandma June after him. "You come back. I'm not leaving just because some jumped-up—"

"Grandma June. Don't."

"They don't have any right to do this. Public safety, my ass. Kicking an eighty-eight-year-old woman and a blind girl out into the street. What the hell kind of safety do they think—"

"And yelling at some pawn about it's going to do any good?" Journey was doing a fine job spiraling into hopeless anger without June's help. "Then what? You gonna write a letter to your MP? Nobody's listening. This is *aliens*. No one cares about whatever little stink you're going to make."

"Who said anything about little? I'm going to tear those—"

"Can you stop? A useless tantrum is exactly what we don't need right now. We've got to figure this out. Help me think. Or pack a bag or something."

"Oh, my baby." A rare tenderness momentarily broke through June's anger. "We'll figure it out. That was never the question." But then the anger was back. "I'm just venting in the meantime."

"Well, don't. We don't have time." Journey's mind was already racing, ideas pushing hard to outpace the fears and almost succeeding. "Worst case scenario, we disappear into the woods. That talk about prosecuting people is nonsense. No way they'll have the manpower to sweep the parks. Hell, give it a week or two, and they probably won't even be paying attention to the houses any more. Either this all blows over and we can move back in, or it all goes to shit and we can move back in because there's nobody left to care."

"Let me think on it a little," said June, and in her voice Journey could already hear the wheels turning. "We'll find a way."

I just found a way, Journey wanted to say, but she held it back. At some level, they were both still adjusting, even though it had been over a year now since Journey had lost her sight and even longer since the mudslide.

They were honest with each other, she and Grandma June, and June would say it if Journey made her. But Journey wasn't sure she could bear to hear it. If June were younger, or if Journey still had her sight, a few weeks in the forest would be nothing. Journey was still sure she could handle it. Pretty sure. But apparently June wasn't, and that hurt. But as long as she didn't make her say it, the hurt was only a little. And bearable.

"What, you don't think you can handle a few nights under the stars?"

"I can take whatever you can," the old woman shot back. "Don't worry your head about me, little miss. Sit down. Listen to your book. I'm going to go see what kind of brilliant escape plan I can rustle up."

"I'm telling you," Journey called after her, letting cockiness temporarily soothe her nerves. "Couple nights in the fresh air and you'll feel like you're seventy-five again."

Chapter Eight

"You boys need a little help?"

Sam looked up to see a man approaching them. He had short, thinning auburn hair, thin-framed glasses, and jeans. A man who looked like he knew what he was doing.

"Um, yeah, actually—"

"We're good, thanks," Gus cut him off.

The stranger gave them a small, ironic smile. His gaze lingered on their crumpled wheels, sweaty red faces, and Gus's vain attempts to lever up the car using his rake poles.

The man walked over and squatted down to examine the wheels.

Gus launched into his explanation. "Just got a little, you know, tire work to do. Looks like the couplers are out. Should be a pretty quick fix."

The man laughed. "I don't think you're going anywhere on this. For starters you're going to need tires, and even if you got a hold of a pair and they were the right size and you had someone to fit them, your rims are beat to hell. What have you been doing? Driving over gravel with no tires?"

"No. We've been driving on perfectly good asphalt, thank you very much. If you'll just get out of my way, I can—"

"Here. Move over." The stranger settled in and began examining one of the bent and dented rims. "Yeah, you're not getting anywhere on these."

"We got here." Gus couldn't, or didn't try to, hide the belligerence in his tone.

Sam jabbed him in the ribs as he turned to the stranger. "Any idea how we can fix it?"

"On a day like today?" The stranger rubbed a hand through his thinning hair, thinking. "Not very likely. You boys do know what's happening, right?"

"Of course!" snapped Gus. "The aliens are coming. Full contingency mode, engage!"

"Something like that," said the stranger with a mirthless laugh. He regarded them both for a long moment, then seemed to make up his mind. "All right. Come on."

"Come on?" asked Sam.

"Come on," repeated the stranger. "Grab your stuff. Might want to move your car out from in front of the pump, too. I'm parked over there." He pointed to an old beast of a pickup truck. "I can give you guys a lift to the next town. Maybe you can find some place to stay, try and get a tow truck out. I don't like your chances, honestly, but it's better than nothing. Best I can do. I'm sorry. I really need to keep moving."

"No. Totally. That's great," said Sam, his stomach churning at the prospect of being stranded in some no-name town somewhere between Iowa and Minnesota. It was better than being stranded at Whatever-U-Need. If nowhere had a middle, this was just about it. "Thanks."

"Unless you've got this under control." The stranger gave Gus a sharp look.

"Actually, yeah. I think we're getting pretty close to getting this figured—"

"Shut up, Gus." hissed Sam. He turned to the stranger. "We'd love a ride. Seriously. Thanks again."

"No problem. We've got to watch out for one another. That's what we're here for. I'm Ronan, by the way."

"Thanks," said Sam. "Really."

"Shotgun!" added Gus.

IT DIDN'T TAKE LONG for Ronan to help Sam and Gus stash their smallish pile of supplies in his truck. Sam limped the car into an out-of-the-way parking spot then the three of them climbed into the truck.

Gus looked into the back while they were getting settled.

"Looks like you're pretty well-stocked."

"Pays to be prepared. You never know when it's all gonna go down."

"What are these?" Gus asked, pawing at some small square bricks wrapped in shiny silver wrapping. "Some kind of supplements?"

"Primal Power masculine nutrition bricks," said Ronan, sounding tired. "Can't stand the things, myself. Taste like chalk. But my sponsors gave me about a crate of 'em, and they do technically contain nutrition. Plus, they pack nice and tight, so here we are."

He put the truck into gear then pulled onto the highway.

"Wait a minute..." Gus looked suddenly thoughtful. "Primal Power. You're not —"

Ronan shot him a guarded look, then turned back to the road.

"Ronan Keats?" gasped Gus.

Ronan tipped his head in a reluctant nod.

"Incredible! This is perfect. I love your show. I listen to you all the time. Oh, my god."

"Thank you," said Ronan quietly.

"I thought you'd be … redder. You know. Shoutier."

Ronan shrugged.

"Oh, man! Do that one about the Masons and how they're poisoning the water to make us all atheists. You know." Gus started a bellowing imitation of Ronan Keats, conspiracy theorist. "The Freemasons and their godless Antichrist religion have been undermining the morals of this country for centuries."

Sam clapped a hand over his face in embarrassment, wishing he could disappear on the spot.

Gus bellowed on happily. "Political infrastructure. Physical infrastructure. Social infrastructure. Trifecta. Get into the grassroots, get into the water pipes, get—"

Ronan waved a hand to shut him up. "All right. All right. That's enough of that."

"But you're so good!"

"Thanks," said Ronan again, tightly. "Where did you guys say you were headed?"

But Gus wasn't to be headed off that easily. "Seriously. Where do you get these ideas? Like, I couldn't make that stuff up if I tried."

"It's not made up. It's the result of years of careful research. I mean … not all of it. But the essentials."

"Really? What parts aren't true?" asked Gus.

"I didn't say they're not true. Just maybe parts are more theory than fact. Some of it I build up a little, present more for entertainment value. But the structure, the underlying ideas, that's all sound."

"Totally," gushed Sam unnecessarily, and wondered why he'd felt the need to say it.

"Seriously?" asked Gus, unable to keep dubious note out of his voice.

"Look, I'll be the first to admit that on the show I go beyond what I've strictly proven. But it's all got a basis in my research. They're theories I'm working out. People enjoy the bleeding edge stuff at least as much as the solidly established core, plus it gives me interesting topics to cover while helping the audience to engage. And they're a great resource for developing exactly those parts I need more data on. My audience has become a critical part of my research. The most significant breadcrumbs have come directly from listeners who have their eyes open, who have access to information I don't."

Gus nodded. "Interesting. Interesting. And this solid core. What would you say is the the well-established center of your" — he waved a vague hand — "you know. Whole thing."

Ronan gave a deep, tired sigh — the sigh of a man who had had to deal with this situation far too many times. He took his eyes off the road for a long moment to pierce Gus with a weighing look. "Mainstream people think all the secret-society, conspiracy-theory, Illuminati-and-aliens stuff is total bullshit. Most of the theories out there are sloppy and they just map out various versions of the same tangled mess — Freemasons and Illuminati and Rothschilds and aliens and what have you. To listen to most of them, you'd think whatever subset they've latched onto is all one big team of secretive people trying to control some nebulous everything for equally nebulous reasons. But that's not how it is."

Sam was fascinated despite himself. This sounded very different than the wide ranging bluster of the Ronan Keats Gus had made him listen to. This was a quiet, thoughtful man who seemed to have given real thought to what he was talking about. It remained to be seen how completely bogus it was, of course, but Sam found himself curious to at least hear him out.

"In reality," continued Ronan, "there are two major blocs that have been in opposition to each other for over a thousand years, with smaller players entering the scene here and there. The reality is very complicated, but to vastly oversimplify, you can center the two blocs around the Masons and the Illuminati.

"Of course, you have to understand those are just convenient labels, easily recognizable signifiers. In reality, they're thoroughly anachronistic, but people are typically less familiar with their forebears, so those terms make convenient labels. The Freemasons were established as a fraternal order in the early eighteenth century, but they're the obvious ideological descendants of a line of inquiry that goes as far back as the Egyptian priesthood, and beyond that to what is represented by the Tower of Babel. They embody the height of humanism, the total confidence that if we think hard enough and try hard enough we can rule the cosmos. They're marked by fierce meritocracy and the ruthless individualism. Might makes right. Look out for number one. Zero-sum game.

"The Illuminati — or more accurately, the Illuminated Brethren — were a secret society established in Europe in the 1800s. The Bavarian Illuminati were an intellectualist movement largely indistinguishable from the Masons early on. But the true heart of what I'm calling the Illuminati arises later, with their turn toward the mystical at the Convent of Wilhelmsbad. This true Illuminati, this search for mystic illumination, is a tradition stretching back to the Knights Templar, the Grail legend, druidic lore before that, and ultimately to the untraceable mists of antiquity. Theirs is a shamanic, interpretive, nature-loving, life-affirming tradition. While the upper echelons are necessarily exclusive due to the rigorous disciplines required to achieve their levels of insight and illumination, the goals are ever outward-focused. They strive always to protect humanity and bring unity."

"So, they're the good guys," put in Sam.

Gus shot him a look. *Really? Good guys and bad guys?*

But Ronan, eyes on the horizon, gave a firm nod. "Exactly. They represent the two sides of a fundamental opposition, a primal duality. One is all about structure, hierarchy, control. One is about integration, cooperation, unity. One is the square, the other is the circle. One is the slabs of concrete paving over the jungle. The other is the grass growing up through the cracks in human civilization. One is ritual magic. The other is nature magic."

"Wait, magic?" interrupted Gus.

"Potentially, yes. It's debatable exactly what that means and how it works. Though both sides certainly purport to bestow great mystical power on their higher-level members. The Masons have been deeply intertwined with Crowley's Satanists, and their research goes all the way back to Babylonian rituals and Talmudic numerology. They're constantly seeking powerful rites they use to exert control and bind extra-dimensional beings of great power to their will. They literally sell their souls for the microscopic chance it will be worth it.

"Meanwhile the Illuminated Brethren seek to open themselves to the spiritual energies at work in the universe. You see it in Stonehenge, the Nazca lines, possibly Easter Island. Medieval alchemy sought the integration of the elements into the philosopher's stone, a symbol of the refinement and purification of all things into an eternal perfection. The Grail quest, the Knights Templar, the aliens mainstream society knows as the grays. In their many manifestations over the years, they seek to be a protective force, manifesting all the potential for good that is inherent to humanity."

"Wait," said Sam. "Did you say the grays? Like, aliens? Little green men?"

Ronan laughed.

"Little green men are a fiction. Or rather, they're a composite conception that probably harks back to some combination of dryad lore, a few folkloric references like the green children of Woolpit, and some sensationalist journalism in the 1950s that captured the public imagination. If there's really anything to that, I'm inclined to think it's in a different direction — more trans-dimensional than extraterrestrial. What you might call fairies. But that gets speculative pretty quickly. There are a few threads that tie into the Grail legend to go on there, but I'd be speaking out of turn to imply there's much that's reliable."

"So you don't believe in fairies. Just the grays," said Gus.

"Something like that. Remember, all of this is a vast oversimplification. But yes, the grays, when they appear, quite consistently show themselves to be a gentle and benevolent presence. I believe they've been working with the Illuminated Brethren and their allies for some time now, equipping them to resist the influence of the reptilians."

"Ooh! Yes," Gus said. "I love this part. Reptilian shape shifters infiltrating the highest echelons of our social infrastructure. The government. The religious establishment. The Boy Sc—"

"Again," Ronan interrupted. "Not all of that is thoroughly proven yet. You have to remember, what's on the show is casting a wide net, letting people enjoy all the suggestive possibilities I'm beginning to uncover. I'd really prefer to keep it to a more sober and well-researched lecture series, but it's a rare lecture series that pays the bills."

"Plus, since when did a lecture series keep anybody this well-stocked in *chalky bricks of masculine power*?" bellowed Gus.

Ronan allowed himself a reluctant smile. "Anyway, it gets tricky pretty quickly when you try to trace exactly how much influence the reptilians have. It probably varies from decade to decade. But there's no question in my mind that there is a strong contingent driving some of the key structures and processes of our social infrastructure."

"Secret shadow government of the lizard folk," hissed Gus in a creepy voice, getting into it.

"So …" Sam hesitated, trying to frame the question. "What exactly have they controlled? According to this theory. Like, what actual laws got passed because the … lizard men or whatever wanted it that way?"

"It's a more subtle thing that. I think it's wrongheaded to attribute specific laws and policies to the reptilians. It's more about the mindset. The tone and method by which things are run. The reptile brain craves routine and ritual. Look at the centers of power and you'll find the pomp and circumstance, the draconic instinct for the hoarding of gold, the craving for order and power and clear hierarchy. It's not a specific political agenda. It's a way of being, of carrying ourselves. To my mind, it's extremely anti-human. It goes against the core of what the creative, diverse, strange, and wonderful beings were made to be. They stifle the richness and newness and individuality that human life and society at its best will bring out. They repress our spontaneous and generous better urges, train us to exclude the outsiders instead of joining together to make a powerful and beautiful tapestry."

"That's really kind of beautiful," said Sam. "I mean, not the part where they're repressing our better urges. But, like, the sentiment about what we could be. And all that."

"I agree." Ronan nodded. "Humanity has so much incredible potential if we could just start to get our act together. That's kind of what got me into this. You know? Any leg up I can give humanity against the forces of darkness. Especially since I'm positioned to figure out a lot more of what's really going on than a lot of people out there. Most people don't have the resources or the mindset. It's a responsibility I don't take lightly."

Sam nodded thoughtfully. He'd always assumed conspiracy theorists were just a bunch of nonsense, and the people who believed in them didn't know how to think and let their crazy biases bloom into full-blown worldviews. He hadn't expected to find Ronan Keats, local celebrity nut job, to be so reasonable, so quietly compelling. So inspiring, even.

And the crazy thing was that knowing he was getting drawn in and even how it was happening wasn't stopping it even a little.

"Okay, look," Gus said. "I'm not saying this is a load of magnificent hogwash. But what would you say to someone who you know …"

Ronan shot him a questioning look.

"You know, who say it's a load of magnificent hogwash. Like, do you think there are actual lizard men out there? Running the government and stuff?"

"Influencing is a better term, and I prefer reptilians, but yes. When you look carefully, the evidence points to a thoroughgoing hybridization between the reptilian and human races. I'm not sure I'd lend credence to the idea that there are purebloods among us, though it's not out of the question. I believe the reality is more nuanced. There's a wide spectrum, lots of different levels of reptilian blood. They've been crossbreeding with us for millennia. Almost everybody's got at least a little by now. But you'll tend to see it clustered in the circles of power."

"But isn't that a little, you know, cuckoo balls? No offense."

"None taken. Believe me. The truth has nothing to hide. If I was just making all this up, I'd have given up along time ago. It isn't easy holding the line against some of the people out there. But listen. It's all right there if you're willing to look, if you've got eyes to see. You know what forms the core of your brain, right? The brainstem, cerebellum, basal ganglia? Do you know what we call that?"

"The lizard brain?" replied Gus, a little reluctantly.

"Bingo. You think that's a coincidence?"

"I mean. I think it's evolution. Right?"

"That's all evolution is." Ronan gunned the engine to take the truck up a sharp rise. "Crossbreeding times a million."

"I guess. So … The original reptilians were dinosaurs? Doing it with humans?"

"Now you're just making fun of me."

"I mean — then what?"

"Look, Gus, you know as well as I do that dinosaurs were not contemporaneous with man. But you look back a few thousand years ago at all the art and all the stories from all the civilizations across all the world, and what do you get? You get dragons. You get the serpent seducing Eve. You get the pictures of semi-humanoid crossbreeds. The Naga. Quetzalcoatl. Wadjet. The Gorgon. Lilith, in some versions. All beings of immense power and authority, revered as sages and queens and goddesses. Consistently associated with wisdom and power and temptation and corruption.

"You get other crossbreeds, too. Centaurs and satyrs and minotaurs and all that, but you'll notice they're all representations of wildness, the opposite of civilization. It's the reptilians who are always gravitating toward the center, toward power."

"So, what? Humans interbred with all kinds of different animals but the snakes became the secret shadow government?"

Ronan laughed.

"Not even close. But I like the way you're thinking about it. That's good. Keep searching. Keep asking questions. But no, I believe there were several classes of inhuman entities — aliens, if you'd like, though I think there's more to it — vying for control of the planet."

"Aliens don't—" Gus caught himself too late.

Ronan didn't say anything, just raised his eyebrows and shot Gus a smirk, then glanced back at Sam, inviting him in on the irony.

"I'm telling you, boys." he said, a cheerful grin stealing across his face. "Everything is about to change."

Chapter Nine

"I'm telling you," Gus said, miles later. "We're going to be in a straight up predator situation."

"Are we the predators are they?" asked Ronan.

"Pshhh. Them, obviously." Gus rolled his eyes and shot a look back at Sam. "You believe this guy? It's like you never saw the movie."

"Oh. Yeah."

"What movie?" said Ronan blankly.

Sam was having trouble sticking to the sci-fi debate. Not that it wasn't fun speculating what kind of aliens they were about to encounter. Normally he'd have been all over that. But the fact was the second they got within range of any excuse for civilization, Ronan was going to drop them off, and they'd be stranded in some tiny town with no plan, no car, spotty coverage, and an armful of badly-packed luggage. Not exactly his ideal start to a post-apocalyptic scenario.

Well, pre-apocalyptic.

"Duh," said Gus. "*Predator*."

Ronan shook his head.

"Seriously? It's a classic! Vintage sci-fi flick. Unstoppable aliens come and hunt the humans. But, you know, awesomer."

Somehow the image of getting hunted by unstoppable aliens didn't do much to improve Sam's nerves. "Why does it have to be a predator situation? Why couldn't it be — you know, benevolent? Cure cancer. Take me to your leader. That kind of thing."

"Are you kidding, Sam? The only reason aliens say 'Take me to your leader' is because they're about to take over the world. What, you think they're trying to join the UN or something?"

"No. I mean, yeah. I mean, you know. Maybe." Sam shrugged. "I mean, why not? If aliens were real, why wouldn't they have some kind of Galactic Senate or whatever?"

"Aliens are real," Ronan said.

"Crap." Sam shook his head. "I keep forgetting. It's so hard to remember it's all actually real, you know? Like, I'm sitting here terrified of how it's going to go down when they arrive, except my brain doesn't even really get that they're arriving, that they're real."

"I'm telling you," insisted Gus. "We've got like five days to live. Or rather, we're the survivors. We'll be awesome. But everybody else, all the sheep — once these buggers show up it's gonna be *pew-pew-pew*," He mimed a laser gun fight. "Toast. Gone. New World Order."

"Not if I can help it," said Ronan.

"Boom!" Gus raised a hand for high-five. "That's what I'm—"

He faltered as he realized just how seriously Ronan was taking it.

Sam was a little surprised, too. He was used to joking around about all sorts of heroics. It was the constant subtext — or would it be supertext? — of his day-to-day interactions with Gus and their comic-store friends. But Ronan was saying it for real, in a gritty, serious, under his breath kind of way. Like a movie action hero. Totally not a high-five moment.

"Wait, what do you mean?"

"Haven't you been listening?" Ronan asked Sam. "Light versus darkness. The age-old struggle. All that?"

"I mean, yeah, but I thought that was, like, the stuff you say for your show. Right? I thought you said most of that stuff hasn't been proven."

"It's hard to prove any of it. Hell, it's hard to *prove* that gravity exists. It's just well documented and fits our other theories well. But there is definitely a struggle between good and evil, and I intend to join it. On the side of the good." His jaw tightened. "Why do you think I'm driving *away* from my bunker?"

"You have a bunker?" cried Gus in ecstasy. "Oh, my God. This is the best ride I've ever gotten."

"Wait," said Sam. "Why *are* you been driving away from your bunker? Wouldn't this be the time to get to it? You know, pretty ASAP? Zombie contingency mode?"

"Zombies aren't real," said Ronan. "Yet."

Gus let out an inarticulate chirp of delight.

"I'm currently headed away from a comfortable and well-stocked bunker in middle Iowa because I'm attempting to establish contact with the Council of Thirty. They are a clandestine organization that has infiltrated most of the circles of power in preparation for an event exactly like this. Perhaps to prepare for this specific event. They are well positioned to minimize the impact to humanity, to do the most good, offer the most protection. And they're recruiting. But it's a tricky path. You have to prove yourself worthy, and a lot of that is figuring out what to do in the first place, how to get in touch with them."

"How do you?" Sam asked. "Get in touch with them, I mean."

"That's what I'm in the middle of tracking down." Ronan rubbed an eye, looking suddenly tired. "Honestly, it's been a rough road. I'm afraid I'm going to have to delve into some areas I'm not exactly comfortable with."

"What does that mean?" Sam pressed.

But Ronan only shrugged. "There's always a cost. Anyway, I guess I'm getting off pretty light. Not that I've gotten very far down the path yet."

A creepy sensation began to crawl through Sam. In his usual happy-go-lucky naïveté, it hadn't even seriously occurred to him to doubt Ronan's good intentions. He seemed like a helpful guy who'd offered them a ride, and that was enough for Sam.

But suddenly he wondered. What kind of a guy went out of his way to pick up dead weight in the middle of a crisis? It was like the opposite of zombie contingency mode, and Ronan struck Sam as the sort to make strategic decisions.

He remembered a few passing mentions of Satanists and rituals. Ronan had spoken like those were the bad guys, but wasn't that exactly what the bad guy would do? Lies and misdirection?

"You don't have to do it," he blurted, then caught himself. "I mean, whatever it is you're talking about. Not that it has to be something bad. Or dangerous or—" He caught himself babbling and cut himself off. "I mean. What do you mean?"

Ronan glanced back with an odd look on his face, trying to figure out what the weird kid was rambling about. He genuinely looked more confused than ... evil or whatever. With any luck, Sam hadn't just grabbed himself the top slot as sacrificial victim.

They zipped past a sign. Homely, Exit 12, 4 miles. Sam's mind started racing with the question of what they would actually do once Ronan dropped them off. He had a brief, horrible mental image of him and Gus standing in the middle of Homely, Iowa looking around like idiots with nowhere to go. Arms bristling with rakes and tubs of jerky and miscellaneous luggage.

Except, who was he kidding? Gus would make him carry everything. And they wouldn't be standing there aimlessly. They would be marching with all the false confidence Gus could muster in an entirely random direction.

"Say," said Gus suddenly, with the light of dawning realization spreading in a grin on his round face. "You're going to be researching, right? Trying to get in touch with the Council of Thirteen?"

"Thirty," Ronan corrected.

"Right, right. I've got the perfect thing." He turned enthusiastically to Sam. "The cabin! He could use the cabin as a base of operations."

Sam had no idea what he was talking about. There was no cabin.

"What—"

"What will he want with our dumpy old cabin?" Gus smoothly interrupted. "Sam, I think you do it a disservice. It's modest, sure. But rich in memories. Plus, it's got a root cellar that could be great in a predator situation."

"I don't—"

Gus turned to pin Sam with what the books call a meaningful look, although Sam had always had trouble telling exactly what it was that meaningful looks were supposed to mean.

"The cabin. Up in Quetico." Gus was trying so hard to

communicate some silent message that it looked like he was trying to poke Sam with his eyeballs.

Sam still didn't know what cabin or where Quetico was but figured he'd better play along before Gus ruptured something.

"Oh. Right. The cabin. In Quetico."

"Where the *night* is full of *foxes*," Gus added, and it clicked.

"Oh! The *cabin*. Yes. Definitely. That cabin."

"You'd be more than welcome, if you want," Gus told Ronan. "It's not much, but it's home away from home. Where the buffalo roam and all that. You could sort of use it as mission central. It's only fair, after you've been so good about helping us out with this ride."

"Which is super cool of you," Sam added a little desperately while his mind worked on overdrive. Were there any mechanics in Homely, Iowa and if so, did any have a tow truck capable of carrying a car with two shredded tires? How much money would it take to convince someone to drive all the way back to a random gas station for a car that was barely worth salvaging? How much would it cost to try? And, under the circumstances, would the mechanic require payment in gold bullion?

Meanwhile, Gus was merrily bubbling on about the alleged cabin. "You could have the loft. Cozy enough. Spiders, sometimes, when we've been gone for a while, but nothing a little broom work won't do away with. You do know how to handle yourself around a broom, I take it?"

Ronan didn't answer. His eyes were fixed on the road, and from Sam's angle, they looked hard, almost angry. But Sam had a bad angle. Hopefully Ronan was just focused on the road.

"And I don't want to brag, but the grill setup is pret-ty solid," Gus bragged. "Epic, you might say."

"Yeah?" Ronan looked at Gus through hooded lids, giving little away. Sam began to feel a queasiness. One he was familiar with. The feeling he got when Gus was obviously going to screw them over with some new idiotic scheme.

He felt a desperate urge to say something, to stop Gus before he went too far. The words pressed up in his chest, an almost physical pressure. But they didn't come out.

"And where is Quetico, exactly?"

"Ontario," Gus said carelessly. "Canada."

"I'll have to have web access. Secure," Ronan added with a sharp look.

"Oh, sure. Secure. Pshaw. We're more secure than … than … well, it doesn't matter what we're more secure than. Super secure. Ultra secure, you could say. Strict fiber hash protocols. You'll be fine. Trust Papa Gus. He won't steer you wrong. Plus, we've got a sniffer on the uplink, triggers a 512-bit mesh if we get any bots."

Sam had to admit it sounded marginally convincing. At least, he assumed it did, to anyone who didn't have much in the way of technical knowledge. Transparent nonsense if you did, of course.

He hoped Ronan didn't have much technical knowledge.

Their driver nodded grimly. "Because privacy is critical."

"Absolutely. Just what I always say myself. Privacy is critical. I was just telling Sam that the other day, wasn't I, Sam? Absolutely critical."

"I heard a 1024-bit mesh is really what you want nowadays," said Ronan evenly.

Another sign went by. Homely, Iowa. 2 miles.

Sam's heart sank. Ronan knew. He had to. He was just messing with Gus now. At this rate, they'd be lucky if he didn't just toss them out of the truck at the top of the exit ramp.

"That's what I heard, anyway," continued Ronan. "You think we can get set up with a 1024-bit mesh?"

"Can we?" Gus gave a low I-don't-want-to-brag sort of chuckle. "1024-bit? Child's play, my friend. Chump change. We can have that set up in no time."

Sam wished that, just for once, Gus would stop trying to bullshit the one person who might possibly be able to do them some good. He was like a pyromaniac for bridges — they were just so pretty when they burned.

"In fact, while we're in there getting that all fixed up, we may as well put in a couple crypto-relays. IBID filters. Maybe even a neural layer. What do you think, Sam? Would a neural layer be overboard?"

Sam tried to resist the urge to clap a hand over his face. There was technically still a chance Ronan hadn't caught on.

They passed by a sign showing the restaurants and lodgings in Homely, Iowa. There weren't many.

"Let me stop you right there," said Ronan. "I don't actually give a rip about your so-called cabin."

"You don't?" asked Gus, taken aback.

"No, because you know as well as I do that you're making all this up on the spot."

Sam's heart sank. This was it. Ronan would drop them off in the middle of Homely, and they would be well and truly screwed.

"I mean, I wouldn't say on the spot, exactly. I mean, not completely on the spot, so to speak."

"I'm sorry," blurted Sam from the back seat. "He just — we just — you know. We really want—"

"What Sam is trying to say, I think—" Gus interrupted, "—is that we are very eager to support your endeavors, and we look forward to working with you if you'll have us. And we could really use someone who knows what they're doing. Like you. Obviously. I mean, we're not exactly the most — I mean, we've got, you know, sort of more of a flair for drama than for actual zombie contingency mode. It looks like."

This last had come out in a grudging sort of hopefulness, unwilling to admit it but, given that he had, hoping that Ronan might choose to join their band. That was how Gus would see it, even though they were very obviously joining Ronan's.

Ronan nodded, inscrutable. The exit was coming up. He slowed.

Sam sighed. He wondered what they could've done differently. Or rather, he knew what they could've done differently. Gus could have not blatantly lied to the guy holding their last thread of hope. But maybe he could have done something. Stopped Gus sooner. Shut down the car spikes. Made himself a home in the aisles of the Whatever-U-Need.

Ronan took the exit. Sam started gearing himself up to stand in a lonely spot with armfuls of luggage or, as the case might be, march confidently in a random direction.

"Another break already? You could just cut down on liquids a little. Or use a bottle."

"Shut up, Gus," Ronan said calmly.

"What? But I—"

"Shut up!" Sam hissed at him.

He finally seemed to get the idea.

"We're not taking another break," Ronan said. "I'm dropping you off."

"You're *what*?" Gus seemed genuinely surprised. Sam finally gave in and clapped a hand over his face.

"I'm glad I was able to help you out with a ride,"

Ronan said with surprisingly little emotion. He didn't seem angry, or like he was relishing this or regretting it. He was like justice personified, neither unkind nor kind, just doing what needed to be done.

"There will be other people here who might be able to help. Maybe somewhere to stay, a mechanic to help out with your car. I don't know what conditions will be like, but you'll have better chances here than back at that stop."

Ronan pulled off the ramp. There was a gas station a bit down the road with a sad little strip mall across from it, and not much else in view. Maybe the rest of Homely was behind the trees.

"You're abandoning us?" Gus cried in outrage. "After you took us away from our car? And from the Whatever-U-Need? You don't think we could have figured something out? It was literally called *whatever you need*." He moaned. "Ronan, Ronan. What did you do? We could have been something, you and me. What about us? What about the cabin?"

"There is no cabin," Ronan reminded him.

"No, obviously. But, like, *metaphorically*."

Ronan pulled into the gas station and parked the truck.

"Good luck, boys."

"Wait," Sam said desperately. "Can you please — I mean, can we—" This was his only chance. He felt an immense pressure building within him. If he didn't get the right words out in the right way on the first try, they'd be finished. And he was so far in his own head, he couldn't get any words out at all.

"Can you what?" asked Ronan.

"Um. Um." *Stop it!* His brain shouted at him. *Say the words!* He looked at Ronan's impassive curiosity. The chance was almost gone.

"Can you help us?" he blurted.

Something almost imperceptible softened in Ronan's face. Just enough to loosen Sam's tongue.

"It's just — we really need the help. And I'm sorry about Gus. He's okay, actually, when he's not being all, you know, like that. I know you don't have to, but *please*?"

Ronan turned in his seat and gave Sam a long, weighing look. Sam did his best to appear …worthy or whatever.

He gave a crisp nod.

"All right. You can keep riding with me, the two of you. But there's a couple rules of the road." He turned to pin Gus with his eyes.

"Oh. Sure. Right. Yeah. Obviously. Sure. Rules of the road."

"You've got to pull your weight. And you have to follow my directions. To the letter. Could be life or death."

"Definitely. That's what I was just saying to—"

"And one more thing," said Ronan.

"Yeah. Of course. Obviously," continued Gus, seemingly sensing he had barely gotten away with something but not yet sure what and was vamping for time while he tried to figure it out.

"I was this close to dropping you off right here in the middle of Homely, Iowa. Just you and your little buddy back there. And you would have been in bad trouble. I'm not sure you get that yet, but it's true."

"Sure." Said Gus. "Totally."

"You know what saved you?"

"Definitely."

Ronan raised his eyebrows and fixed Gus with a stern look. He shrank back in his seat.

"I mean. I mean, not exactly. I mean —"

"What saved you is the fact that this guy" — he jerked a thumb at Sam — "was willing to apologize for you, and that you" — he raised a pair of fingers half an inch apart — "*barely* managed to admit you weren't being honest and might need some help. I'll give you another chance, but I'm not going to work with people I can't trust. Don't do it again."

"Totally," said Gus, still floundering. "Sure. Yeah. I get that."

"I'm serious, Gus." Ronan pulled back out onto the road. "I make my living seeking out the truth. Don't bullshit me."

"I feel like that's kind of a strong word for—"

"Shut up, Gus," muttered Sam tightly and for once, miraculously, Gus shut up.

Chapter Ten

"Would you like twenty dollars?" Nestor asked the stranger, flashing a broad, rather yellow-toothed grin that was far too childlike for his white-stubbled seventy-something face.

The question was clearly not one the stranger expected to encounter unprompted while pumping his gas. His eyes flicked to Nestor's ride, an old-fashioned Cadillac with an oddly-extended rear. "Is that a hearse?"

Nestor nodded. "Got it as a gift. Third one in a row. But seriously, can I bless you with a twenty?"

"You don't have twenty dollars to give him," said Nestor's friend, Thor.

"Sure, I do." Nestor fished eagerly around in his wallet until he triumphantly pulled out a twenty dollar bill. "Ha!" He handed it to the confused stranger. "Here. God wants to bless you today."

"Um, thanks?"

"Sure." He leaned toward the stranger confidentially. "Keeps you loose, you know? You gotta give it away before you start depending on it too much."

"I don't mean you don't have twenty bucks in your wallet," said Thor, his words coming out thoughtful and deliberate as he caught up with the conversation. "I mean you shouldn't give away money you can't afford. The good Lord provides, but he doesn't do it willy-nilly." His Norwegian lilt made it *villy-nilly*.

"You don't have to—" The stranger sounded uncertain, halfway handing the twenty back.

"Keep it," said Nestor. "There's plenty more where that came from. Do you like burgers? Go get a nice juicy hamburger. Read the Bible. That's where Jesus would be. Down at the hamburger joint, having a cold beer and talking shop."

"Okay, uh, thanks."

"I'm only saying," continued Thor, "if you're going to be giving away twenty dollars here and twenty dollars there, the farm is in a lean year, and the combine always needs a tune-up."

The stranger turned to Thor. "Do you want the twenty?"

Nestor also turned to Thor. "Do not worry, saying, 'What shall we eat?' or 'What shall we drink?' or 'What shall we wear?'"

"Sure, sure," intoned Thor. "But also, 'Go to the ant, thou sluggard.' You want to get really loose, you could write me a check as big as you want. I wouldn't even cash it until Monday, just to give Him a little time to pay you back."

"Here," said the stranger, thrusting the bill at Thor. "Help yourself."

"Thank you." Thor took the bill with a small, stately nod. He turned a slow wide smile on Nestor, then lifted his hands and looked to the heavens in thanks. "The Lord is my shepherd; I shall not want."

Nestor ignored this. He addressed the stranger again.

"That's good. You're getting more generous already. Feels good, doesn't it?"

"I don't know." The stranger was nonplussed. "I mean, it wasn't even mine in the first place, So—"

"Exactly! You're getting it. Here." Nestor fished around in his wallet and pulled out a few crumpled fives and tens. He gave them to the stranger without bothering to count them. "I told you, God wants to bless you. And don't even think about it," he added to Thor.

The stranger laughed nervously. "Okay. Well, thanks. I think I should…" He pointed a vague hand at the gas tank that had long since finished pumping, then turned away.

After the stranger drove off, Thor turned to Nestor. "Surely a kind enough gesture, but how will you pay for your gas now?"

Nestor looked him in the eye and grinned. For a long moment they stood eye to eye, two tall white-haired men alone in an empty gas station lot. Nestor waggled his white eyebrows, still grinning. Thor rolled his eyes.

"Sure, sure. But only a few gallons." He unscrewed the cap of Nestor's gas tank and began pumping, keeping a hawk's eye on the spinning numbers. "I'm keeping some of this." He waved the twenty at Nestor. Then his stern expression gave way to a sly smile. "Hamburger money."

Nestor let out a great guffaw. Then he sobered as an old familiar tug arose within him.. "Let's finish up. I think I've got somewhere to be."

Thor continued watching the spinning numbers, then released the handle with a precise move. $8.02. He let out a mild grimace. "You're just now remembering that? We really need to get you a calendar. I should have gotten you one before now. They have some with puppies on them. It's very cute."

"No, no, not like that." Nestor paused for a long moment until Thor finally looked up at him. Nestor raised his eyebrows meaningfully.

Thor sighed. "This isn't going to be like last week, yes? When you drove me two hours out into the country for an ice cream sundae and returned right back?"

"Do you have anywhere better to be?"

"Just because I don't have a specific appointment or task doesn't require me to wander off on a frivolous drive for ice cream."

"You could use a little more frivolity in your life," insisted Nestor. "And besides, just because you don't know what that was about doesn't mean there was no purpose to it."

"Okay, then. What was it about?"

"Haven't got the foggiest idea." Nestor's face split into a wide yellow grin. "But that doesn't mean there's no point to it, either. Anyway, hop in."

Thor settled himself in the passenger seat of the old hearse. "You get these *tullebukk* ideas and the rest of us have to come scurrying after you like little tiny white bunnies. Scurry scurry scurry."

"That is an adorable mental image. That I would get on the calendar." Nestor turned the key. The hearse gave the reluctant grinding growl its old engine always made while it got used to the idea of driving one more time, then finally started up.

"Very funny," said Thor, his lilting accent offsetting the dour note in his voice. "But funny doesn't plow the ground."

"The ground is still thawing. You've got nothing better to do. What, are you gonna sit in the dark and listen to your old radio?"

Thor pursed his lips. "I think I would light a candle or two."

Nestor laughed merrily. "No. You're coming with me. This will be a good one. You'll see."

"Where are we going?"

"Somewhere along Highway 53."

Chapter Eleven

It was getting on toward evening when Ronan decided to stop at a gas station to stretch his legs and refuel.

"But it's an alien invasion!" Gus protested. "DEFCON Five. Zombie contingency mode. This is when you drive straight through the night. Never surrender. Never look back."

Ronan ignored this and took the exit.

To be honest, Sam was also a little surprised that Ronan was willing to stop for something so mundane as stretching his legs. It seemed like an awfully casual approach to the apocalypse.

"I'm telling you," Gus insisted. "We keep taking stops they're going to get a jump on us. We're going to be sitting ducks."

"There is no them," Ronan calmly pointed out. "This isn't a race. And much as everyone's treating it as a crazy zero-sum scramble, the survivors will be the ones who pay attention, stay careful, make the right moves. Not the ones who keep rushing around just to be doing something. And besides, there's a reason pilots and surgeons and air traffic controllers have mandatory off hours."

"We're not surgeons. We're warriors. Survivors. You think Marines take stretch breaks in the middle of a mission?"

"Look," said Ronan. "The human brain needs its breaks, and so does the human body. Push too hard and you got sloppy, error-prone. And that's a bad scene. *Especially* in high-stress conditions."

"But DEFCON Five! We'll rest when we're dead."

"I'd rather rest while I'm still alive. And besides," he added as he parked the truck and hopped out. "I think you mean DEFCON One. DEFCON Five is the least severe rating."

That shut Gus up.

"Dude," Sam said. "Stop antagonizing him. We're screwed if he decides you're too much of a hassle."

"Oh, he won't," said Gus darkly. "Don't you worry your pretty little head about that, my young Padawan. I have a plan. Come on."

Gus scrambled out of the truck then yanked Sam along on a walk around the parking lot, well out of Ronan's earshot. He then ambled along with his hands in his pockets, elbows cocked, and whistling carefree. "Act casual."

Sam jerked free. "Stop that. I don't know what you're doing, but … don't."

"Listen," muttered Gus out of the side of his mouth, still trying to act casual. "Here's what we're going to do."

Sam clapped a hand over his face, the started massaging his temples. "Gus. Please, please, please don't screw this up for us. Please. Seriously."

Gus sniffed. "I'm offended, Sam. When have I ever screwed things up for — Don't answer that, actually. It's time for us to focus on the future, Sam. That's all behind us, and I think you'll agree this is our greatest heist yet."

"No! No heist. No — whatever you're doing. We got a second chance. Let's just ride with him for a while. Help out if we can. You know? And like, not die. Or end up abandoned in a parking lot with an armful of rake poles."

"Rake poles," chuckled Gus. "You're a charming young man, Sam. But do you know what your problem is?"

"My taste in friends?"

"A lack of vision. Ronan has no need for dead weight. He'll want us to contribute. He said as much. And contribute we shall. And that's not all."

"It's not?"

"If my plan succeeds, Sam, we will not only 'not die,' as you put it. We will bend him to our will. We will overcome, young Samuel."

"Don't call me that."

"We will bend this Ronan, if that is his real name, to our will."

"Wait, what?"

"He'll even think it's his plan. I'm telling you, Sam. This guy is looking for someone to get him on the true path, right? Find the breadcrumbs he's supposed to be following to his made up whatever?"

"I mean, that seems like a kind of dismissive way to—"

"I don't care! Listen. Desperate times and et cetera. Right? We'll plant some breadcrumbs for him to discover, and those delectable little morsels of misinformation will lead us straight up to—"

Sam saw it just before Gus said it. They said it at the same time, Sam with a groan, Gus glowing with enthusiasm.

"Quetico, Ontario."

"Exactly!" preened Gus. "Now you see it."

"Gus. This is horrible, terrible idea. Seriously. We can't—"

"We've got him wrapped around our little finger, and he doesn't even know it yet. I mean, we don't yet. So obviously he doesn't. But we will! And *then* he won't know it."

"We're not doing this, Gus."

"And once we're in Quetico, we drop him like the chump he is. And then, my friend, make-out city."

"We're not doing any of that. Look, Gus. This isn't about getting you a kiss any more. Forget Night Fox. This is about survival. Don't you get that? Ronan's our one chance. You can't throw it away for—"

"I can and I will, young Sam. I will throw it all away. After all, if we have no make-outs with the fair Night Fox to look forward to, why are we even here?"

"I *don't* have make-outs to look forward to."

Gus waved this off. "You're getting off the subject. Here's what I'm going to need from you, Sam. When I give the signal, you create a diversion."

"I'm not ... We're not doing this. Okay? No diversions."

"Now," Gus said stroking his chin theatrically. "All we need is a data tab. Something to really bring home the fiction of the Man Behind The Curtain, feeding our doughty hero the clues that will lead him to—"

"What we need is to stop screwing with Ronan before he throws us out of his truck on the side of the highway. The only reason he didn't dump us in the first place is—"

"Because I managed to smooth things over with him."

"Because I apologized for your bullshittery!" shouted Sam in a burst of frustration, then quickly glanced around in embarrassment at a few bystanders as he realized what he had done.

"I don't know, man. Bullshittery seems like a strong word for—"

"Bull. Shittery," Sam insisted. "I'm telling you. The second he figures out you're lying again, we're on the side of the highway and SOL."

"Then maybe stop broadcasting the ruse to the entire world," Gus murmured. He began looking around. "No, this is good. We just need to bring it home."

His eyes lighted on a minivan fueling up nearby. A skittish-looking man with red hair, a baseball cap, and a Twins tee was leaning against it, poking at a data tab. As they watched, he slid open the door and stowed the data tab in the back seat.

"Perfect. Get Ronan back in the truck and await my signal."

"What?" Sam cried. "What's perfect? Nothing is perfect. I'm not awaiting any … you know. Signal. That's—"

"Shh-shh-shh." Gus patted him on the shoulder. "You'll be fine. I have every confidence. Just go get Ronan. Trust me."

"I don't trust anything about this. Really, Gus. I've got a bad feeling about this. Whatever you're doing, it's … not good."

"That's right. You just keep telling yourself whatever you need to. Just go get Ronan. Wait in the truck. It will all be over in a few—"

He drifted off, carefully eying the minivan in search of the right moment. The man finished fueling the minivan then headed toward the building. Gus's eyes lit up.

"Okay, perfect. Go. Go. DEFCON Five."

"You mean DEFCON One."

"Nope. Five. Everything is under control. Go. Go."

"Gus, I really don't think you—"

But Gus was already darting over toward the minivan. Sam hesitated, torn between the desire to stop him from his plan — whatever it was — and the desire to get Ronan and get in the truck. Get head start for when things inevitably went south.

He took a couple faltering steps after his friend, but it was too late. Gus was crouching beside the minivan and trying the handle of the sliding door. It was unlocked.

Gus turned and threw the horns with a cocky smile at Sam.

"Oh, man," moaned Sam. He tried to catch Ronan's eye from across the parking lot then, failing that, started waving his arms to get Ronan's attention. Still nothing.

Gus began to scrounge around in the minivan's back seat. The man in the baseball cap turned back toward the van. Maybe he'd forgotten something.

"*Gus*. Abort. Abort." Nothing. "Ca-*caw*."

Gus kept rummaging, then surfaced with the data tab. He raised it triumphantly over his head. Minivan guy saw it and shouted, "Hey!"

"Ronan!" called Sam in desperation. Ronan turned and Sam jerked an urgent thumb back toward the truck as Gus called, "No names! No names!"

Ronan's head snapped around. He took in the scene and started running over.

Meanwhile, Gus had managed to tumble backward out of the minivan and was trying with only moderate success to scramble to his feet. The man, who was more athletic than Sam had realized at first, dashed back to the far side of the minivan and dove into the front seats to start scrounging for something.

"Gus! Get out of there!" called Sam, starting to run toward Ronan's truck as well.

Gus started crab walking backward, still too rushed

and panicky to get on his feet. The man was yelling profanities, and Sam, glancing back, saw him straighten up, finally having found what he was looking for in the front seat.

A shotgun.

"I said get the fuck away from my minivan, asshole!"

"Oh, crap—" cried Gus.

"He's got a gun!"

For an endless moment, Gus froze — one hand still down in half a crab walk, the other reflexively clutching the data tab.

"Come on!" Sam dashed forward to yank Gus to his feet.

Gus shouted, too, but it came out as a terrified battle cry of pure panic.

The man cocked the shotgun.

"Get the fuck back."

He continued screaming. Sam joined him. Gus finally managed to let go of the data tab and Sam helped him scramble to his feet. The man menaced them with the shotgun.

So this is how I die, thought Sam with sudden clarity.

"Stand down," boomed Ronan's voice.

Sam turned back, startled at the irresistible authority the words carried.

Ronan was pointing a hunting rifle directly at the man's head.

"Get in the truck," he commanded the boys in a tight voice.

Gus said, "It's fine. We're cool. I was just working on acquiring—"

"Shut up. And get in the truck." Despite his thinning hair, gold framed glasses, and only modestly-muscular build, Ronan was suddenly terrifying.

Sam tried to scramble toward the truck, tugging on Gus's hand. But he stood transfixed, caught between the man's shotgun and Ronan's booming voice, the data tab still lying on the ground in front of him.

"Everybody stay cool," Gus croaked. "I'm just gonna—"

He began leaning very slowly, very deliberately toward the data tab.

"Get the fuck back! Don't make me shoot you. I'll do it." The man looked like he was trying to gear himself up, talking himself into what he knew he might have to do. Just another regular guy forced into awful, unpredictable circumstances. Same as them.

That didn't mean he wouldn't shoot.

"Gus, come on."

"Truck is about to leave, boys," snapped Ronan. "I think you want to be on it."

Finally seeming to get the picture, Gus abandoned the data tab and started making his way toward Ronan's truck.

"Lower your weapon," Ronan commanded.

Sam didn't bother to look back and see whether the man had complied.

"Move!" bellowed Ronan.

The boys scrambled into the back seat of the truck as fast as they could and wrestled their way through a tangle of rake poles and luggage.

In a single smooth move, Ronan lowered his rifle and hopped into the driver's seat. He put down the gun, slammed the door and was peeling out backwards before Sam had managed to get his butt into a seat.

"What the *hell* was that?" shouted Ronan as soon as they were back out on the highway. "You trying to get us killed? I should have left you behind."

"And abscond with our supplies? I see how it is. Not so

much of a white knight after all, eh?"

"Shut up," snapped Ronan and Sam in unison.

"Geez. I was just trying to help. No need to bite my—"

"*Help?*" Ronan was incredulous. "What the hell kind of help was that?"

"You may have been too busy waving that gun around to notice. But I very nearly managed to acquire us a data tab — completely unconnected to any of our names or identities, I might add — that I could have used to give us a big head start finding your precious breadcrumbs. If *someone* hadn't interrupted my rather delicate procedure."

"Interrupted you!" Sam's voice was more shrill than he preferred. "That guy was waving a shotgun at you! He could've blown your head off!"

"Duh. What do you think I was talking about? You don't think getting your head blown off counts as a distraction? Geez. I didn't realize you were a Shaolin monk of ultimate focus."

"Goddammit," Ronan swore under his breath.

"Look, I'm sorry," Gus protested. "I was just trying to help. Take one for the team. The mission first and all that."

"Shut up. I'm not talking about you," growled Ronan.

"What? Then what are you—"

"That moron is coming after us."

"What?" They turned in their seats, wrestling momentarily with the tangle of rake poles and other miscellaneous equipment.

"Holy crap!" cried Gus.

The minivan was in hot pursuit, maybe eight cars back and swerving madly to and fro in an effort to catch up.

"Pedal to the metal!" cried Gus. "Warp factor nine!"

"Quiet!" Ronan gunned the engine and the truck lurched forward.

Sam peered out the back window. The minivan fishtailed around a dark blue sedan and started honking at a long red eight-seater.

"He's gaining on us!" Gus cried.

"How?" shouted Ronan.

"I don't know! Maybe he … souped it up or something. Put a turbo on the transmission or whatever. I'm not a car guy!"

Ronan laid on the horn as he hit a patch of traffic. The cluster of cars ahead didn't respond, except for a couple retaliatory honks. The minivan was gaining fast.

"Holy crap!" shouted Sam. "The guy's leaning out the passenger window. And he's—"

A muffled bang sounded behind them.

"—got a handgun!"

"This is just shameful," protested Gus. "Moral fiber nowadays. Complete shambles. Piece of my mind."

Sam realized Gus was starting to hyperventilate. Berating societal ills was one of Gus's coping mechanisms.

"No standards at all. Whoo. Absolute. Heh. Disgrace," he panted.

"Out of the way!" Ronan leaned on the horn and gunned the engine in frustration.

"Ronan?" quavered Sam. "He's about to … *you know*—"

"Grab the rifle," ordered Ronan.

"I mean. I don't really … I mean I haven't …"

"Just grab the goddamn rifle!"

Sam fumbled his way around the luggage and reached into the front passenger seat.

"Do I just … I mean is it—"

"Simple point-and-click interface!" snapped Ronan. "I thought you were a nerd."

"Yeah," Sam chuckled nervously. "I just didn't … I mean I don't—"

"Just lean out the window and point it at him. He'll get the idea."

Ronan leaned on the horn again, but Sam noticed he wasn't yelling at the other vehicles. He'd always wondered why people bothered to yell at cars. There was no way they could hear you. This Ronan was shaping up to be an unexpected kind of guy.

"Move!" barked Ronan.

"Oh! Right. Sorry."

Sam opened his window and pointed the rifle out. That wasn't right. He needed to point it back at the minivan behind them.

He stuck his head out, but that made it difficult to fit his arms through, much less the bulky rifle. He started trying to wrestle it up past his head, but quickly aborted at the sight of the barrel pointing at his throat. He tried flipping it around, but pointing it into the car didn't seem much better. He wondered where the safety was.

"Just give it here," snapped Gus.

"No!" shouted Sam and Ronan together.

Gus with a rifle was not going to improve the situation.

"Just give it!" Gus insisted, a slightly whiny note slipping into his voice. "Come on, Sam. They're gaining on us. DEFCON ... probably Two. Maybe One. Ronan, are we at DEFCON One yet?"

"Shut up!" Ronan laid on the horn again, but it was useless. There was nowhere for the cars ahead of them to go.

The minivan was less than two car lengths behind them and gaining. Sam could practically see the fire in the man's eyes as he hunched over the steering wheel.

"All right," Ronan said, concluding a discussion nobody else had been having with him. "We're gonna have to go for it."

"Go for what?" asked Sam, just as Ronan swerved hard left.

The truck darted over the shoulder, dropped down into a shallow culvert with stomach-lurching suddenness, and bounced out the other side. Ronan gunned the engine and they began bouncing through a fallow field, all dirt clods and flattened yellow stalks.

"Wahoo!" howled Gus. "That'll show 'im!"

"He's still coming," said Sam.

"What?" shrieked Gus.

The minivan had swerved after them without missing a beat. It looked like he'd blown a tire going through the culvert, and one of the bumpers was dragging, but the maniac behind the wheel had gone into pure bloodlust and was burning up his engine in the chase.

"Gun!" Sam shouted.

The driver behind them was aiming a bouncing pistol in their general direction as he steered with one hand.

"You've got to be kidding me! Here, give me that." Gus swiped at the rifle and managed to grab it near the middle.

Sam tugged back. "Gus, no!"

"Here, just let me—"

Within moments they were wrestling for the rifle. Ronan shouted something from the front seat, but Sam was too busy shouting himself to catch it.

A gunshot boomed from behind them, followed by another.

"Give it!" grunted Gus, yanking again. There was a deafening explosion, then Gus began screaming. The rifle dropped to the truck floor.

"You idiot!" shouted Ronan. Behind them, the minivan was losing ground. Gus continued screaming, and Sam saw blood pouring onto the seat cushions.

"Um!" Panic sluiced through him. "Blood!"

"A-a-ah!" Gus screamed. Sam's eyes darted from the blood still flowing to the minivan out the back window. Another couple shots from the pistol outside, muted and small compared to the rifle blast that had left his ears ringing.

"What do I do?" he bellowed over Gus's screams.

"What?" Ronan yelled back.

"Quiet!" Sam shouted at Gus.

He thought of the moments in all the movies where one person slapped the other to get them to stop. His hands wouldn't do it. He settled for grabbing Gus by the shoulders and giving him a good shake.

"Quiet!" he snapped again.

Gus kept screaming, bouncing around as Sam shook him and the truck sped through the field.

Sam realized the blood was coming from Gus's leg. The screaming and bouncing continued.

"Damn it," Ronan swore.

"I think it's his leg!" Sam shouted.

"I think it's my leg! My leg! A-a-ah!" Gus began sobbing.

"Just shut up a second," Ronan ordered.

He didn't.

Sam glanced back and found the minivan surprisingly far behind them, now honking in impotent rage. The man was still waving his pistol outside the driver's window, but Sam was pretty sure they were out of range. Probably. He didn't really know what pistol range was. He wondered whether he should have been counting shots.

"I think we can stop," Sam said. "They're not chasing us any more."

Gus perked up, and a blessed silence filled the truck as he finally shut up for a second.

"Nope," said Ronan grimly.

"What?" cried Gus. "Why? What's going on?"

"Because you shot the brake line, you damn idiot."

The Jeep hit another bumpy patch, and Gus started screaming again.

"Shut it!" snapped Ronan with such authority that Gus actually did.

"Does that mean we can't brake at all? Or, like …" Sam's voice cracked, suddenly shrill. "You know. Just a little?"

"Not at all, Sam," Ronan answered tightly. "No brakes."

"So just bounce to a stop or whatever," said Gus.

"Shut up, Gus," snapped Sam and Roman in tandem.

"Hey, I'm the one who got shot in the leg."

The engine growled, and the truck bucked forward as Ronan gave it another rev.

"What are you doing? I thought you said the brakes are out!"

"A, you don't get to talk," Ronan said to Gus. "B, we're in the middle of a huge field. You want to walk all the way to the next road?"

"How am I supposed to walk with a shot-up leg?"

He gunned the engine again. The pickup bounced over a particularly big bump.

Gus screamed.

Ronan smiled grimly. "Then I figure we'll get to the edge of the field and then bounce to a stop like you said."

"Should we be, like, stopping the bleeding or something?" Sam asked.

"First aid kit in the back. Get some gauze and press it down. I'll take a look once we get to a stop. Or we can just let him bleed out and be short one idiot."

"*What?* I was protecting us! I'm the only one who fired a shot back there. If it weren't for me we'd be—"

Again, they said in unison, "Shut up, Gus!"

"This is a conspiracy! I was trying to save your butts. If it weren't for me we'd still be —"

Sam snapped, "Oh my god! Can you seriously not hear yourself?"

"I can hear myself plenty! Just because you have no idea how to point a rifle out of the window and — OW!"

Sam had found some gauze and mashed it perhaps a little harder than necessary against Gus's wounded leg.

"Okay, here's how this is going to go," said Ronan. "Gus, you don't get to talk anymore. Talking privileges are revoked until further notice. Sam, apply pressure to the leg and try to keep him still."

"And not get too much more blood on the seat?"

"Unless one of you has a spare brake line on you, that's the least of our worries."

The truck hit a rough patch, and he gunned it again to keep them moving.

"Ow!" cried Gus. "Stop that."

"When we get to the edge of the field, we'll be near the junction with Farm Road 524. If there's no traffic, I may try driving as far as I can manage safely, but we can't count on that. In either case, we'll be stopping soon. At that point, I'll take a look at his leg and get it stabilized. Gus, are you going to be able to walk?"

"I don't think so. It's really bad." In an unexpected British accent he added, "Just a flesh wound."

"Which is it?" Ronan asked Gus. "Really bad or just a flesh wound?"

"Oh. Very bad. I thought 'just a flesh wound' was something you said. You know, when you get shot." Gus was trying to puff up his chest, but you didn't get street cred for shooting yourself due to total stupid incompetence.

Ronan said, "It's not. Stop messing around."

Sam was pleased to see Gus deflate.

"Do you actually have a legitimate reason to think you can't walk, or are you just …" He waved an angry hand back in Gus's general direction to indicate the whole unfortunate conglomerate of Gusness.

"Yes, I have a legitimate reason, thank you very much. I just got shot in the actual leg, as you may recall."

"You can still walk if it just went through. Did it hit any bone? Or hit your foot or your ankle?"

"I think it …" Gus petered out, his words giving way to a soft uneasy moan. His face paled.

"New plan," Sam said hurriedly. "Gus, just look out the window. Don't worry about … I think he got hit in the shin."

"Damn." The pickup had hit a mercifully smooth patch and rumbled gently along, slowly decelerating as Ronan rode the line between giving it more gas and keeping the speed low enough that they could still coast to a stop in fairly short order if the need arose. "I'll have to take a look at it, but there's a chance you've got bone fragments in there, in which case you want to minimize movement."

"No kidding! You think I'm gonna"—Gus waved at all the nature around them—"just traipse around through the backwoods of Minnesota with *bone fragments?*"

"You might still be fine. Like I said, I have to take a look. Anyway. We'll have to try and flag down a ride when we get there. Then I want you two transferring provisions. I'll tell you what we need and the order we need it depending on the space available. If we can't get a ride, which is probably the more likely scenario, you guys get to wait in the truck while I go for help."

"You're going to leave us?" asked Gus.

"Feel free to hit the road on your own if you want. No skin off my nose."

"What if we just …" Gus broke off, apparently trying and failing to come up with an alternative plan.

"I just told you the plan, all right? What I don't need is second-guessing and confusion. Especially from the guy that just screwed us."

Gus was about to protest, but Sam managed to redirect his attention by accidentally shoving the gauze a little too hard against his leg again.

By the time they reached the edge of the field, Gus had stopped even trying to blame anyone or complain about his leg, much less propose new plans. In fact, Sam was getting worried. Gus was looking pale and a little faint. Just how much blood could a guy lose before it was a real problem? By the look of the back seat, Gus had already lost a few square feet or so. Sam was a little way into the conversion from square feet to quarts before realizing he was just distracting himself so he didn't have to think about how bad things were getting.

But the truth was, it seemed unlikely a stranger would pick them up. Especially with everybody panicking about aliens. Things were turning dog-eat-dog awfully fast.

The farm road was narrow, barely two real lanes winding through the fields. It was paved, but so old and dusty and lonely looking, it may as well not have been.

The road was curvy enough that it would have been a terrible idea to try to make further progress without brakes. Instead, Ronan stayed in the field and turned parallel to the road so the their last burst of speed could peter out. The pickup rolled to a stop with a depressing finality.

Sam then realized exactly how stranded they were. He'd never really been in fields before, not in the proper farm sense of the word, and after a lifetime in cities and civilization, the wide open spaces with nothing but nature felt lonely, desolate.

He got out of the truck then helped Ronan get Gus out for closer examination. It wasn't good.

"You boys have put me in a tight spot," Ronan said as he examined Gus's wound. "He's not going to be able to walk on that for a while, and you really want to get him some proper medical attention soon as possible. If infection sets in, that's gonna get really bad, really fast."

"But there isn't anyone around," said Gus.

"Yeah, no kidding." Ronan rose and scanned the horizon. He shook his head, his calculations apparently coming to nothing. "All right. Here's how it's going to go. Because I'm a decent person, I'm going to let you wait in my truck if you want, and if I find someone who can help I'll bring them back here. You may each eat one of these"—he grabbed a nutrition brick—"every twelve hours. That's minimal, but it's enough."

"Twelve hours! How long are—"

"Shut up, Gus. If you don't hear from me within sixty hours, don't expect to. If I do manage to find help, we'll try to get you stabilized, and then we go our separate ways. After that, if we ever cross paths again, keep moving or it's gonna get ugly. Sam, help me get him situated."

"Totally." Sam trotted over, trying to show hustle without getting in the way, terrified of antagonizing Ronan any further. "Sorry. Um." He swallowed, suddenly desperate for anything to say, any words that would get him past the terrifying coldness in Ronan. "Any idea where we are, by the way?"

Ronan gave a tight shrug. "The hell should I know? Somewhere off Highway 53."

Chapter Twelve

Gus turned to Sam with that eager, sneaky look he got when on the edge of some really stupid scheme, like stealing all of Ronan's crates of supplies and walking quickly down the highway with them. Of course, with the shape his leg was in, he probably meant for Sam to carry him or some idiot nonsense. But he'd barely opened his mouth before a pale blue Cadillac hearse appeared over the top of a small hill nearby.

It pulled to a stop between Ronan and the boys and gave three friendly toots of the horn.

Ronan turned back to watch as a tall, skinny man with short white hair and a rather goofy grin got out of the driver's seat. After a moment, an even taller, muscular, dour-looking old man got out of the passenger side.

"I thought I might find you boys here. Hop in. You three look like you need a ride."

Ronan's eyes narrowed suspiciously.

"What do you mean, you thought you might find us here?"

The grinning stranger didn't answer. He peered at

Ronan for a long moment, still grinning, then waggled his bushy white eyebrows.

Sam glanced Ronan just in time to catch a look of startled understanding, which he quickly stifled. "Oh." Ronan gave the old man a meaningful look. His eyes shifted to the other passenger, the one who wasn't grinning. "Yeah," he said a bit too casually. "I could use a ride."

"We're coming too," said Gus.

"Great! Hop in. I'm Nestor, by the way. Nestor Olfend. This is my buddy, Thor Halvorssen."

"Cool name," Gus said.

The man acknowledged this with a small nod but said nothing.

"I'm Gus."

"Sam."

"Ronan," said Ronan, giving Sam and Gus the evil eye.

Sam wondered if it was okay for them to be barging in on the ride. It seemed like Ronan had only barely made his peace with getting Gus set up on the side of the road before putting some distance between them. It was probably a good idea to give him space. Maybe sharing a hearse wasn't such a good idea.

But they all climbed in. Sam ended up in the middle, stuck between Gus and Ronan as Nestor and Thor resumed their places in the front.

"So, where are you boys headed?" Nestor asked.

Ronan answered. "Opposite directions, actually. I was just heading north to try and find what I need to put in a new brake line and to get Gus stabilized and mobile. Then these boys were about to head anywhere else."

"Well," said Nestor, either cheerfully ignoring or unaware of the angry undercurrent in Ronan's answer. "I can do north. In fact, that's where we just came from. Beautiful little town by the name of Lake Peculiar."

"That does sound like a beautiful little town. I think we might like to see it. What do you think, Sam? Then Ronan can head wherever else he wants to."

"Hold on," said Ronan. "It looks like we're all stuck going in the same direction for the time being. Maybe let the grown-ups talk for a minute, all right, kid?"

By now Nestor had turned the hearse around and was driving back the way he had come. North, apparently.

"I take it you two had a reason to come find us?" asked Ronan, again adding a meaningful emphasis to his voice, although Sam still couldn't tell what the meaning was supposed to be.

"I guess you could say that," said Nestor. "I think if you pay attention, there's a lot of little missions out there. Ways to make the world better. Little connections. You know what I mean?"

Ronan glanced over at Sam and Gus with a bit of a smirk. *See? And you boys thought I was out to lunch.* "Yeah. I think I do."

Again he gave Sam and Gus and knowing look, and with a sinking feeling, Sam realized Ronan thought their sudden benefactors were part of the conspiracy. The Cabal or the Council or whatever it was.

Which they obviously couldn't be. Could they? He clearly had to be wrong. That stuff was total hogwash. It had to be.

Then again, how had Nestor and Thor known exactly where to find them?

"Truck broke down, eh?" asked Nestor. "Bad time for it."

"It didn't exactly break down—"

"Ow," Gus cried, cutting Roman off. "My leg! It's really acting up."

"Your leg?" Ronan repeated.

"I really think I need to rest for a little bit. You think we could all just … you know, stop talking? About what happened back there or whatnot? So I can rest my leg?"

Sam shot him a dubious look, which he returned with studied innocence.

"Up to you," said Nestor. "But I am going to want to hear all about you sometime soon. Deal?"

Gus looked nervous. "I guess?"

"Great. You drink coffee? My treat."

"Okay?"

The hearse settled into silence, except for occasional happy sighs and mutters from Nestor in front. Sam wondered if he had one of those cutting-edge implants that took the place of a wireless earpiece. He didn't seem the type, but then, Nestor didn't fit any of Sam's expectations.

"Home sweet home!" Nestor declared a little under half an hour later as they drove past the sign welcoming them to Lake Peculiar, population 827.

"*You're here now, you betcha.*" Sam read as they drove past the welcome sign. As mottoes went, it kind of left something to be desired.

"You sure are!" Nestor cackled as if it was some kind of private joke.

Thor did not. Instead, the dour old farmer surveyed the back seat, as if tallying new mouths to feed. "All right, Nestor. You found your little stray ducklings. What are you going to do with them now?"

For a long moment, Nestor and Thor locked eyes. A silent argument passed between them. Sam figured Nestor had been assuming everyone would stay at Thor's house and Thor was assuming nothing of the sort.

"Well," said Nestor, apparently reevaluating on the fly. "First things first. We've gotta get that leg looked at for you, don't we, Gus?"

"About time," said Gus.

"Let's see if Pastor Ellie's got a spot for you."

"Pastor Ellie?" asked Gus, looking a little scared.

"Oh, she's great. Just great. And there's plenty of room in the parsonage. Good, big beds. Central location. Dr. Olson can come by and take a look at you any time you need it. Perfect."

"You're not going to dump a crowd of strangers on that little girl out of nowhere, are you?" asked Thor. "The good Lord knows she's got enough on her mind as it is these days."

"I'd hate to be a bother." As soon as he said it, Sam wondered what else he could possibly be. It wasn't as if he'd brought along a hotel room in his duffel bag.

"Nonsense! Nonsense. No bother at all. You two can stay with our interns over at Fresh Fire," Nestor said. "Should be plenty of space. You two can be bunkmates."

Sam glanced uneasily over at Ronan. Did sharing a bunk count as crossing paths?

"I'm not … I mean. I don't —"

"What's that?" asked Nestor from the front seat, stretching up to peer at Sam in his rearview.

"I can't sleep around interns." It wasn't true, and Sam wasn't sure where it had come from, but it seemed as good a reason as any. He swallowed. "Bad experience. You know. Back in the day."

"Well, that's not true," Nestor said. "Why would you go and say thing like that?"

"Nestor," warned Thor quietly.

"You ignore this stuff, you stay trapped. I'm trying to help the kid. I've got a good feeling about this one. I don't want him to go to waste."

"What do you mean, go to waste?" The conversation was taking an unexpected turn, and Sam didn't exactly like the sound of it. In fact, he didn't even know what to think about the sound of it. "How did you know that wasn't true?"

Ronan snickered. "You know, you two aren't as sneaky as you think you are."

Sam's gaze darted to Gus, who opened his mouth in protest, but Nestor beat him to it.

"That's true, but that's not how I knew. You didn't want to stay at the intern house, and you were too embarrassed to give your real reason. That's pretty obvious to anybody with a little life experience. And that's fine, no shame in it. But here's the thing, Sam. Do you mind if I tell you some things? Maybe a little personal? We're all friends here, right?"

Curiosity and dread wrestled inside him. Not that Nestor knew anything personal about him, of course. Still. Sam didn't like the sound of that at all. "Sure. Yeah."

"You're a good kid, Sam. Always have been. Even without trying, and you try awfully hard. But here's the thing. You're desperately scared people won't like you, and that keeps your hands tied. It hobbles your potential and your freedom and your joy."

Sam began to feel incredibly claustrophobic, trapped in the back seat of a moving car. He willed his mouth to make Nestor stop. But of course, he didn't. Sam was a nervous, nice, non-confrontational kind of guy, and once you were as old as Nestor, you could probably see that in seconds. But it was the first time anybody had spoken to

Sam so directly about it, especially in front of others. Especially in front of Gus.

Nestor continued, friendly and unstoppable. "You're in a cage, Sam, but you can start breaking the bars if you want to. Know how? You say the thing you're most scared to say. Start asking the questions and telling the truths you've been avoiding. Even if it means some unpleasantness. Even if it means a fight, or someone not liking you for a little while. Although I don't think you need to worry about that, Sam. They'll come back around."

"Okay," Sam said uncomfortably. "Thanks."

But Nestor didn't stop. "You think I'm just making generic observations that shouldn't hit this close to home inside you. But they are, because this is more than that. I'm going to give you your first three steps to freedom, all right, Sam?"

It's okay. I don't want my first three steps to freedom, Sam said desperately in his head. His mouth stayed resolutely frozen shut.

"This thing with the intern house. Be honest about why you don't want to stay there, then ask me if you can stay at my house instead. That's the first one, and it will be hard, but not too hard. Like when you started to deal with Gus about this girlfriend situation. You wish you had one, too. But it's deeper than that. You wish for once you could be the one who got the quest."

"How the hell did you—" But then Sam caught himself. "I mean ... I don't ... How are you doing this?"

"But that's not really Gus's fault, is it? Talk it out with him. Come to terms with it. You made a good start, now keep going. Be honest, but work through it. Got it?"

Sam swallowed and nodded.

"Anyway. Second one's interesting. There's going to be an awkward silence. You're going to want to break it and not want to break it at the same time. When that silence comes, break it." Nestor jabbed a finger in the air for emphasis.

"Totally."

"Third one's up to you. Keep your eyes open and you'll see it pretty soon, I imagine. Your friend is going to do something you just can't stand by, and when you see that…" Again Nestor stretched up to meet Sam's gaze in the rearview. For the first time since Sam had met the perpetually-smiling old man, a deep sadness darkened his eyes.

The silence drew out until Sam could no longer take it. "When I see it, what?"

"Simple enough. Don't just stand by."

Nestor's eyes were back on the road, and it felt like a spell had broken.

Sam sat reeling, trying to make sense of how the old man had known all of that. Even the first part had hit harder than it should have, and there was no way he could know about the girlfriend and the quest.

Was he some sort of spy? Or an advance scout for the aliens? It was insane, of course, but two days ago, believing in aliens at all would have felt insane.

"Um." It took Sam a moment to get his mouth working again. "How did you know all that stuff? Seriously. You're kind of freaking me out a little."

Nestor gave a little shrug. "I don't think you'd believe me yet. But that's all right."

"I might." But the more Sam thought about it, the more he realized Nestor was probably right. Either that or it would turn out disappointingly mundane. Or creepy. That was always an option.

Gus said, "It's cool. I mean, we get it. You did some little trick. A good magician never tells. Whatever."

"But that was real stuff," Sam said, still not sure what to think.

"It's like you've never heard the word 'cold reading.' Psychics pull this kind of thing all the time. With all due respect," Gus added.

Nestor grinned, seemingly unoffendable.

"Don't write it off too quickly," Ronan said. "There's a lot of ways a person can know that kind of thing."

"You mean like ... surveillance?" Sam was starting to wonder if he should have taken his chances by the side of the highway.

"Sure. Remember what I was telling you about. There's your evidence right there."

Sam should be drawing some sort of conclusion, but both the data he was trying to make sense of and Ronan's implied theory were so outlandish, he didn't even know where to start.

"Aliens?" asked Gus, coming to the rescue.

Ronan nodded. "There are several different sources of telepathic connection. Sometimes even the practitioners don't know the real story. They call themselves psychics, say God spoke to them, call it visions. And they're entitled to their own theories, of course."

"Very kind of you," Thor said gravely.

"We're here," crowed Nestor, as if it was the most exciting thing that had happened to him or anyone else all day. He hopped out to hold the door for Ronan and Sam. "After you."

Chapter Thirteen

"Let's just take a little time and really just … really soak in the Lord's presence."

It had been almost twelve minutes since Pastor Jonathan had said that. Not that Pastor Ellie Jensen was counting. That would be unseemly. It was Pastor Jonathan's turn to lead the inter-church prayer meeting that met weekly in the drafty fellowship hall of the First Lutheran Church of Lake Peculiar, and Pastor Ellie was determined to support a diversity of styles.

The meeting was a chance to build relationships, and God knew she needed all the good ones she could get. Even if his turn to lead the meeting always seemed to take a turn toward the mystical in ways she couldn't exactly get behind. The lanky man was the pastor of Fresh Fire Pentecostal Church out on the edge of town, and he did his best.

She snuck another look at her watch and tried to keep 'soaking,' which she took to be a sort of spiritual reflection of a somewhat less guided variety than she was used to.

Her mind drifted back to the problem of Doris and Dotty. Dorothy "Dotty" Bjornssen and Doris Koenigsdottir

JACK RAVENHILL

had been best frenemies for the last thirty or forty years. At least, that was Ellie's best bead on the situation.

She knew her efforts to win them over were about as unlikely to work as their chocolate chip cookie bars were to fund the renovations of First Lutheran Church's crumbling Historic Old World Slate roof. But she had to make the effort. Without Doris and Dotty's support — she suspected that, in the end, there was no such thing as the support of Doris *or* Dotty — a new pastor had no chance of any sort of real success in Lake Peculiar.

Doris ran the town knitting circle with an iron fist, and Dotty held court over the neighborhood Gardening Association. Each had privately confided in Ellie that the other was terribly unsuited to the job, although, as both added like a little protective charm against unfriendliness, "goodness knows she means well."

Goodness knew a lot of people meant well in Lake Peculiar. Thor Halvorssen, the Norwegian bachelor farmer who lived a little northwest of town and came in every week for the church service before indulging in a cheap cut of steak at the Peculiar Grill House — arguably the single vice in his extremely sober life — had warned her about his best friend Nestor, who attended the odd little Pentecostal church and was apt to drop anything when he "got a notion" that God had told him something.

"Oh, yah, he's a frivolous man, always skipping off anytime he's got a notion that the Good Lord is planting the idea for grown men to go driving off for ice cream villy-nilly. But goodness knows he means vell."

And the banker, Barty Olufsen, had warned her about Pastor Jonathan Morgenstern of the odd little church as he gave her a ride to the monthly ecumenical prayer meeting. The four pastors of the four churches on friendly terms held this meeting each month at a corner booth at the

Peculiar Grill House. The three other pastors, Ellie soon found, spent the same hour eying them from three separate nearby tables as they consumed their morning steak and eggs and strong black coffee.

"Very nice man. Really very kindhearted. Some strange notions, certainly. Doctrinally, perhaps a little unusual. Though goodness knows he means well."

And, no doubt, the parishioners said it to one another about her. At the meetings of the knitting circle, while they ate Doris's shortbreads and made scarves and needlepoints to sell at the extremely well-meaning fundraisers they held whenever they accumulated enough square footage of reconfigured yarn.

And at the meetings of the Garden Association, where they spent the long winter evenings enjoying Dotty's special mulled cider and knitting socks and mittens while they waited for the ground to thaw enough for some gardening.

Members of her congregation no doubt said it to one another after Sunday service, when they all met at the Peculiar Grill House for cheap cuts of steak and still left Pastor Leif's seat empty. Pastor Leif had been a mountain of a man who died as he lived, preaching a rousing sermon of fire and brimstone before repairing to the Peculiar Grill House for a double portion of — to Ellie's mind — rather worryingly inexpensive meat.

All of them, no doubt, assured each other that for all of the young new lady pastor's inexperience and misplaced enthusiasm and notions, goodness knew she meant well.

And, goodness knew, she really did.

"… We ask all these things in your name. Amen. Thank you, Jesus. Thank you, Lord."

Pastor Jonathan brought the meeting to a close. The dozen or so attendees groggily rose and gathered their things. The quiet chatter of conversation filled the high-ceilinged fellowship hall.

Pastor Ellie opened her eyes, congratulating herself on making it through another PJ Special. She immediately caught herself and threw out that thought as unbecoming.

Above them, the wind whistled ominously through some unseen cracks in the roof. Across the little circle of wooden chairs, Barty Olufsen was fussing around unnecessarily with his briefcase, as if a briefcase took a lot of gathering up, and refusing to meet her eye.

She sighed and tried not to think uncharitable thoughts. She was not looking forward to this meeting. And by the looks of it, neither was Barty.

Pastor Jonathan came over to give her a clammy handshake, then halfway through seemed to think better of it and made a partial transition into a hug. He was a sincere man, with musty corduroys and a head of prematurely-graying hair. Another one she did her best not to think uncharitable thoughts about. He was, so far, one of her strongest supporters, presumably because it was a pastor's job to be welcoming even when nobody else exactly felt like it.

"Still having trouble with that roof, I guess," he observed with a sympathetic half smile that might have indicated some kind of a joke.

Ellie managed a tight smile, doing her best to warm it up. The roof was the last thing she wanted to talk about. How was she supposed to respond to that, anyway? It was a non-statement. Ancient roofs didn't spontaneously get better overnight. "I guess."

"Let me know if you need any more tarps. I can have Todd and John Mark bring some over and help you put them up."

"Sure. Thanks. Whatever you've got." She cast desperately about for a conversational destination. "Any idea where Nestor is? He usually comes to these."

Jonathan shrugged with a limp little smile. "The wind blows, and no man knows where it comes from or where it goes."

"No kidding. Hey, I've got a meeting with Barty. Okay?"

"All right. Just let me know if you want those tarps."

Leave it to Jonathan to make her actually look forward to the meeting with Barty. Sometimes the frying pan was awkward enough to make the fire look downright cozy. She caught Barty's eye from across the room and gestured toward her office.

A few minutes later, after they had settled into the office and shut the door, he said, "Good prayer meeting."

"Listen, Barty, I know you've pushed this to the limit, but if you can just get us a couple more weeks—"

"I wish I could." He didn't meet her eyes. "But the head office is really breathing down my neck on this one, Ellie. There's nothing I can do."

"You guys don't even want this building. Trust me." She smiled ruefully. "That roof is a liability. The whole place is coming apart at the seams. And it's not like it's corrugated metal up there. The stonework, the gargoyles, the stained glass. We're talking real historical significance, complex restoration work. You foreclose on this place, it's gonna cost you a fortune. Really, Barty. Did you tell them?"

He gave her a sad little smile. Ellie didn't envy him. The Lake Peculiar branch of the First National Bank was a friendly little operation where the tellers knew their customers by sight and you could usually slide past the industry formalities. Barty was the branch manager, but in the summer, it was a regular occurrence to see him out front with his suit jacket off and his sleeves neatly rolled up, mowing the bank's tidy patch of lawn with an old rolling mower. In the baking months, the bank was always filled with the smells of a plate of cookies or brownies or bars that one of the tellers had baked and left out for customers, and every other Thursday it was Barty's famous fudge ripple bars.

He was, in short, just the sort of man you want running a tiny local branch, but not the kind of man you want foreclosing on the historic Lutheran Church building at the center of his town and its social life.

And while Ellie felt bad for the friendly little man, and a little guilty about taking advantage of his reluctance, it was her job to save the building the best she could, and if that meant applying a little gentle pressure to buy them more time, then that's what she would do.

"I know, I know. Believe me. I don't want to be here any more than you do." Barty still couldn't meet her eye. "But the fact is, you've already had three extensions. It's out of my hands at this point. You know if it were up to me—"

"Did this happen when Pastor Leif was still here?" Ellie asked with a gentleness calculated to disarm him and bring the jab more effectively home.

"Oh. Well … that was different. You know. He'd been a member of the community for such a long … and he and Vice President Johnson up in St. Paul go back such a long way." Barty seemed to recover himself. "But that's not the issue. Any leeway Pastor Leif may have gotten is really an even longer extension of the grace period, if you think about it. This needs to be resolved, one way or the other. I'm sorry. You know as well as I do—"

He faltered, waved a hand back at the big fellowship hall where they'd had their little prayer meeting, and where the town regularly congregated for meals and harvest festivals, youth nights and bake sales.

"I love this building. And this church. I don't want to … but there's nothing I can do, Pastor."

Barty looked up at her so miserably that her heart almost broke. But what was she going to do? Hand over the keys because the man was sad? Have her congregation sit on the park benches and the snowy grass in the little town square every Sunday morning? No. Ellie served a practical God, a God who came alongside those who fought for what was right, who comforted those in need. He could comfort Barty. And she would do her best to fight for her congregation and the town.

"I tell you what." She cut past his uncertainties with all the pastoral authority she could muster, but softened it at the edges. She was pretty, and for all the obstacles being an attractive young female pastor put in her way, she'd learned a smile here and a touch of affection in her voice there could unlock many doors posturing and bluster wouldn't touch. "We've got the fete coming up in a few days. It will be one of our biggest fundraisers yet. Let's see how that goes, and maybe we can go from there."

Barty smiled uncomfortably. "Now, Pastor. You know as well as I do there's no way——"

"Let's just wait and see. Have a little faith, Barty."

"With all due respect, Pastor. You're not going to raise six figures with a bake sale and a dunk tank."

"And a sausage stand. Don't forget the sausage stand. People love their sausages."

Barty let out an uncomfortable little groan. "You're making this hard for me, Pastor——"

Curses, you've unmasked my cunning plan, thought Ellie wryly. "Look, I'm not saying we can get the whole debt paid off in a stroke, but who knows? Maybe somebody will be moved to give more generously than we expect. It might be enough for a good-faith gesture, buy a little more time with your bosses. I know you don't want to shut this building down, so why not give us a chance to give them what they want, right?"

"I really don't think—"

"It's one week, Barty." She tempered her sharp tone with that sweet smile and melty eye contact that made men of a certain age do stupid things. The classic one-two punch. "You can turn off your voice mail for that long. They'll think you went fishing or something."

"One week?" He sounded doubtful.

"One week." She rose to signal the end of their meeting. "Thanks, Barty. I really appreciate this."

Chapter Fourteen

Ellie stepped outside, gearing up for the next bit of the gauntlet.

She approached the bake sale table with some trepidation and smiled at the two little old ladies behind it.

"Good afternoon, ladies. How are sales?"

"Well, I think everything is looking quite lovely," said Doris. "Everybody just has to get their hands on Dotty's delicious oatmeal raisin cookies."

"But Doris's bars are the real winner here," Dotty protested. "People just can't seem to get enough of them."

"Well it was my grandmother's recipe, you know," Doris said modestly. "Been in the family for so long, I don't know if anybody can really take credit for it anymore."

"Well," said Ellie, eying the Saran-wrapped goodies spread across the tabletop. "I think I'll just have to try something here."

For all their false modesty, she half expected them to start hawking their own treats at her. Having the pastor buy one of yours was probably worth extra points in whatever strange little game they were playing. In fact, it occurred to her that it might be more diplomatic to buy a brownie. Mrs. Gunderson, a harried mother of three, had bought them at the local grocery store and dropped them off on her way by.

This was considered amateurish, at best. And really, when you got right down to it, perhaps downright insulting. But goodness knew she meant well. In fact, now that she thought about it, Ellie wondered whether buying one of the brownies would, in fact, damage her standing more than picking Doris over Dotty or vice versa.

Then, in a sudden resurgence of common sense, she realized that she was vastly overthinking the purchase of a simple baked good and, while it would certainly help her gain credibility with her new congregation to have one or the other of them — or preferably both — on her side, it was probably uncharitable to assume that they'd be so petty as to give or withhold their support over whose treat she'd picked.

"These brownies look good," she said.

Dotty and Doris exchanged a look, the raised eyebrows on mirror image old lady faces speaking far more eloquently than any words would have. Not that Dotty or Doris would have said those words right out loud anyway. Ellie had been quick to learn that when the Synod moved her in from the East Coast. One didn't say unkind things in the Midwest. One remained Nice.

Still, the ladies had managed to make their opinion pretty clear even without the use of words.

"Of course," she amended, "I'd be foolish to pass up the chance to enjoy these delicious treats you ladies have worked so hard on."

Which brought her back to the impossible question of which one she was supposed to select. They peered up at her with sweet smiles and steely eyes, waiting to pounce on her decision.

"Maybe one of each," she said.

"Now, now, dear," said Doris. "No need to try to spare Dotty's feelings like that."

"And you can't go buying double treats all the time," added Dotty. "Pretty young thing like you should keep an eye on her figure. Give the men in town a reason to keep coming to church," she added slyly.

"Dotty!" cried Ellie, masking genuine shock with playful outrage. "You're so bad."

"Dotty was quite the beauty back in our day," observed Doris. "You want the men eating out of the palm of your hand, you just listen to her advice."

"Of course, in the end you only need one," said Dotty. "Are you seeing anyone yet, pastor?"

"I saw you canceled your slot in the fellowship hall next Thursday," Ellie said hurriedly. "Everything all right with the Ladies' Circle?"

"Oh, sure," said Dotty. "It's just that it gets so drafty in that fellowship hall, and now with the leaks in the roof and the stormy season coming—"

"It gets harder when you're older, like we are," continued Doris almost without a break.

Ellie wondered fleetingly if the two elderly friends might be twins separated at birth and reunited at a bake sale.

"But don't trouble yourself about it, Pastor. We'll just take turns hosting it until those repairs are taken care of."

"You will?" Ellie tried to keep the disappointment out of her voice, spin it as gratitude at their willingness to go above and beyond. But in truth, this was a severe blow.

It has been observed that if a man is the head of the house, the woman is the neck, and she can turn the head any way she pleases. In much the same way, the Ladies' Circle was the strategic heart of the First Lutheran Church of Lake Peculiar.

If, in the course of tea and pastries, the conversation of the Ladies' Circle happened to turn toward the Christmas pageant, and if it was felt that the list of songs was insufficiently traditional — not that anyone would complain about such a thing, of course, but if it happened to come up — and if the consensus arose that wreaths would be nice instead of banners this year, these ideas would percolate through the town in a manner which modern physics might find it profitable to examine.

The ladies would talk with their friends, and those friends would mention it to their husbands, and soon, even though nobody would be so bold as to complain or suggest changes, it would become common knowledge that the song selection was in need of an update and the decor was going to be wreaths this year. And somewhere in the planning process, there would be an update to the song selection, and when the decorating committee did its shopping, they would find themselves returning with wreaths.

It was, of course, an open question if and when the ladies were going to invite Ellie into their midst. She knew, instinctively but certainly, a grudging invitation would be worse than none at all. But in the meantime, the next best thing was to be the pastor in whose fellowship hall the Ladies' Circle gathered.

The ladies could drink the church's coffee and sit on the church's padded folding chairs and develop those little bonds that food and habit build. There she could walk past on her way to or from some small bit of business and exchange greetings and brief pleasantries with the ladies. Never pry, of course, nor overstay her welcome, but for one as sensitive to these things as Pastor

Ellie, ten seconds of pleasantries was more than enough time to gather the room's mood, alongside other valuable intelligence.

And, of course, most importantly, Pastor Ellie's office adjoined the fellowship hall, and with the door left ajar — for which pastor would isolate herself from the needs of her congregation by shutting them out of her office? — she could hear not everything, but *enough* of the Ladies' Circle proceedings.

Forewarned was forearmed, and once the meeting broke up, there was always the possibility of coming out for cordial goodbyes and the careful nipping in the bud of the occasional more extreme decision.

But if they had started meeting at Doris and Dotty's homes …

"I really wish you'd told me," said Ellie. "I hate for you to go to all that trouble. Maybe if we move in some space heaters or—"

"Oh, no, no," said Dotty, waving this off with a kindly smile. "Don't trouble yourself. You just worry about getting that church ship shape again, and we'll be back before you know it."

"A pastor must have so much on her mind without a bunch of little old ladies cluttering the place up, anyway," added Doris. "We'll get out of your hair and leave you to the important parts."

"What do you mean?" Ellie cajoled. "You ladies are the most important thing on my agenda." *And I wish that was just flattery*

The ladies waved this off, looking modest and pleased.

"At least let me get in on the hosting rotation," said Ellie. "I need some people over at the parsonage now and then. The place is so empty, so much bigger than I need. I just rattle around in there."

"Oh, we couldn't ask you to do that, Pastor," said Doris.

"Really. I want to."

"Now Pastor, don't worry your pretty head about us. We'll be fine. You just keep your mind on getting settled in. Get in with the people who get things done around here."

And how exactly do you expect me to do that if you keep cutting me out? she wanted to scream. Put on a fake mustache and join the Sons of Canute Lodge? At least there they'd just swat me on the ass and tell me to mind my own business.

"Well, just let me know if you change your mind."

"No, no. You don't want to trouble yourself about us," said Doris or Dotty. Ellie was starting to get a little too tired to care which.

"Pastor Ellie," said a voice behind her. She turned to find herself a little closer than she would have expected to Nestor's broad yellow grin. He was accompanied by Thor Halvorssen and a couple men she didn't know, a middle-aged man with thin glasses and a watchful bearing and a younger man, probably in his twenties, who was skinny and uncertain looking.

Her heart sank a little.

"Hi, Nestor."

"I need you to do me a favor. If you don't mind."

"Sure," she said, trying to keep the tiredness out of her voice. She turned back to Doris and Dotty. At least she was out of the frying pan. "If you'll excuse me, ladies."

"Of course," said Doris sweetly.

"Duty calls," added Dotty.

She turned back to Nestor. "How can I help?"

"This young man's friend needs a place to stay."

"Oh. Sure." Ellie tried to master her confusion. She supposed she was going to end up hosting the friend, whoever these strangers might end up being, but she wasn't entirely sure why Nestor had come to her with this. He didn't even attend her church, though he was friendly enough. Friendlier than some of her own congregants, really. And it wasn't as if she didn't have room. The parsonage seem to have been designed on the assumption that a good pastor would follow the biblical injunction to be fruitful and multiply.

"He's going to need medical attention," said the nervous looking young man. "I'm Sam, by the way. Sorry."

"Ellie," she introduced herself, wondering what the young man was apologizing for.

"I'd keep him myself, or toss him in with the interns, but Sam here is gonna be on my pullout couch, and we're so far out on the edge of town —" Nestor let the sentence trail, but she took his meaning. Lake Peculiar was extremely convenient if you lived in small cluster of relative civilization around Division Street, and awfully inconvenient once you hit the outskirts. Especially if you needed medical attention.

"Of course. What's wrong with him?"

"Acute idiocy syndrome," muttered the man with the glasses.

"He got shot in the leg," said Sam.

"Oh, no!" said Ellie.

"Self-inflicted," added the man in glasses. "He'll be fine. He'll probably need to stay off his leg for a bit, and we'll need to get him looked at by a doctor, if possible."

"Sure. I'm sure Dr. Olson can take a look at him."

"Thanks," said Sam. "And he's fine, really. Once you get to know him."

"Oh. Good." The reassurance made Ellie feel anything but reassured.

"He's over here in the car." Nestor began leading the way back to his hearse, and Ellie followed, already thinking logistics. He could have the guest room — that was easy enough. Meals should be fine as long as he wasn't too picky. The parsonage served as an ad hoc meeting space for a few groups, but as long as he was willing to keep his distance if the conversations went in a confidential direction, that shouldn't be a problem.

Nestor opened the back door of the hearse to reveal a heavyset young man about the same age as Sam. "Gus, you'll be staying with Pastor Ellie."

"On-shawn-tay," said the passenger, emerging gingerly onto one foot. He looked around with a proprietary air. "Yes, I think this will do nicely. Quaint. Even rustic. But not without its charm."

Ellie raised an eyebrow. "Thanks."

"Sam, Ronan," said Gus. "I suppose we'll have to divide up the supplies equitably. Can I trust you to be fair?"

"Well, since they're all my supplies—" began Ronan.

"None of that, now," Gus cut him off. "I would've hoped we were past that kind of petty individualism and quibbling. This is a the dawn of a new age, Ronan. Galaxy mind. You've got to think beyond yourself. Big picture, man. Big picture."

Ronan's jaw tightened.

"I'll get your suitcase," Sam said hastily.

"Go bag," Gus corrected.

Ellie smiled and wondered whether it was too late to renounce the pastorate.

Chapter Fifteen

Sam sat in the back seat of Nestor's hearse, trying not to breathe too much of Ronan's air. They were on the way to the intern house, and Nestor was chattering happily about his grandchildren and a bubble gun he'd been inventing for them, plus a trip to Israel he was planning, not seeming to mind that Ronan and Sam were sitting in tense silence in the back seat.

Sam still wasn't exactly sure where things stood with Ronan ever since the incident that had left them on the side of the road. From the moment Ronan said if their paths crossed it would be trouble, they'd spent an awful lot of time sharing a back seat, and Sam only narrowly avoided sharing a bunk in the intern house.

The intern house, it turned out, was little more than a sort of miniature prefab warehouse on the grounds of Fresh Fire Pentecostal Church, which was itself a trim little building with a light industrial look, like it had been a used car lot or a small warehouse or something in a former life.

The interior was similarly plain, but welcoming. Somebody had set up a hammock in one corner, along with a few beanbag chairs and an old couch and an armchair arranged on a big ratty section of carpeting. Crammed into another corner were three bunk beds in uncomfortably close proximity, and nestled into a third corner was a little kitchenette and a long communal table.

They walked in to find a half-dozen college boys at the table, eating soup. They looked up and hailed Nestor's arrival with a ragged cheer.

A couple of them hopped up and dashed over to greet the newcomers, projecting great grins ahead of themselves like energetic mini-Nestors.

"Hey, I'm Todd," said one.

"John Mark," said the other.

Ronan shook their hands a little skeptically. "Ronan. Pleasure."

"You'll be staying here," said Nestor. "These boys will take good care of you. Won't you, boys?"

This brought another chorus of enthusiastic agreement. Ronan's face hardened, as if enthusiastic church interns were how *they* got you if you weren't vigilant.

"I'm seeing six boys and three bunk beds," Ronan noted.

"I can take the hammock," said one of the interns from the table.

Another called, "I can sleep on the couch."

"I can always sleep on the floor if we have to make room," John Mark added confidentially.

"Soup?" offered Todd.

Ronan's brow furrowed, perhaps running the calculations and discovering there was no reasonable way to decline.

"See? 'Do not neglect to show hospitality to strangers,

for by this some have entertained angels without knowing it.' You all set?" Nestor added, turning to Ronan.

Ronan surveyed the room, and Sam could practically see his brain spinning through the strengths, weaknesses, opportunities, threats.

"Yeah. Looks good." He turned to give Nestor a firm handshake. "Thanks for everything. Can't tell you what a help this is." A small ironic smile crept onto his face. "Just to be clear, though," he told the interns. "Not an angel."

NESTOR'S HOUSE was a small one-story bungalow with a lived-in feel and a homey smell that reminded Sam of his grandparents' house, somewhere between scented candles, cut wood, and a touch of mildew. Despite the grandma-house smell, wood paneling, and the honest-to-goodness shag carpet in the living room, Sam found himself feeling immediately at home when he walked through the door. It was a peaceful sort of place. Sam wasn't really into puzzles, but it felt like the kind of spot he could have lost himself for hours working on one and sipping from a cup of tea if he had been.

"Welcome," Nestor said, sweeping along arm out to wave Sam into the house ahead of him. "Blessings and peace as long as you are here."

"I … Thanks."

"This will be where you stay," added Nestor, beginning to wrestle with the pullout bed hidden inside a ratty over-stuffed couch. "Little on the old side, but you're young. It will be fine."

"Totally." He looked around, getting the feel of the place.

"Help yourself to food. Anything you want. We've always got oatmeal in the—"

"Um, about that stuff you said in the car," Sam said suddenly. "Did you … I mean, how did you—"

"Oh, don't worry about that," said Nestor, clapping Sam heartily on the back. "I'm sure we'll get to all that when the time's right. Come on. Let's get your bags in here."

Chapter Sixteen

Journey and June sat at the table in dismal silence, trying to think of solutions.

"Cass?" asked Journey without much hope.

"Not a chance," said June a little sadly. "They put her in a home a few months ago. And besides, she's all the way in Vancouver. That's a hell of a trip when you've got no car and the infrastructure is breaking down. I wonder if Bill could help us get my old bike running."

"Yeah, and I could ride a unicorn," said Journey.

The silence stretched between them.

Journey heard Grandma June get out of her seat.

"June?"

"Just a minute, babe." The stairs creaked as June began climbing upstairs.

"Where you going?" Journey called after her.

"Just have to check something," replied the old woman.

Journey's mind turned back to the problem at hand. They didn't really have much in the way of relatives, certainly not anybody close enough or properly equipped to offer them any kind of help. Cass was June's sister.

Journey suspected she was starting to succumb to dementia.

"June?" She called again after some minutes had passed.

"Be right down, babe," Grandma June called down.

The frustrating thing was how much harder it was going to be without her sight. She knew her way around the staff settlement, and she had her home and workplace set up, her routines in place. Moving somewhere else was going to be like stepping off a cliff, leaping out into the unknown void.

She heard the creak of the stairs, and then June was back. "What was that about?"

"Oh. Probably nothing. Just a shot in the dark. You think of anything?"

Journey shrugged. "I could hit my forums. Kindness of strangers and all that. Maybe — no. That's nothing. There's no way this actually pans out."

"Listen, babe. You got something, don't sit on it. No idea too crazy at this point."

"Yeah." Journey rose with a sigh and headed upstairs. "Nothing too crazy."

Chapter Seventeen

Sam sat in an uncomfortable little wicker chair in Gus's room in the parsonage, trying to think of something more to say. Gus lay in his bed, staring at the ceiling, his leg in a more proper splint and bandage after the town doctor had gotten a chance to look him over at Pastor Ellie's request.

The muted tick-tock of a grandfather clock seeped in from the hallway.

"So. Not too bad, then," Sam tried.

"I've been given a cane, Sam. I'm an invalid. I've been relegated. Have you ever been relegated?"

"Um. I'm not … Maybe in some sense of—"

Gus hunched up in bed to glare at him.

"No," Sam quickly corrected himself. "Totally."

Gus gave a satisfied nod and eased himself back down.

Sam had been spending the past fifteen or twenty minutes trying to think of things to say and, when he occasionally did think of something, saying it. Unfortunately he was no good at coming up with topics that would actually spark conversation, not in situations like this, and each of his utterances had fallen limply into the air and drifted back into the same heavy silence.

An old timey trumpet blared on Gus's phone, like a herald about to announce something important.

"Ooh!" Gus straightened and scrambled for it.

The strange notification was a huge relief. It gave Sam a natural question to ask and, better yet, one that had nothing to do with Gus's injury or their failed road trip or any of the wide minefield of topics Sam was so busily equating.

"What's that about?" he asked, handing Gus the phone.

"WarDuster. I left the notifications on just in case." For a long moment, Gus peered at the screen, first reading the message, then apparently stricken. Then he slumped back to the bed and tossed the phone carelessly back onto his night table.

"Damn. We were so close."

"We were? What do you mean? Close to what?"

"It's Night Fox," said Gus. "She wants to see us. Like, not even in a maybe we could get coffee sometime kind of way. She sent her address and everything."

Sam brightened. "That's great! That's like exactly what we wanted, isn't it?"

"Yeah. Except she's in Canada."

"So? We made it this far."

"That was before *somebody* shot me in the leg," said Gus.

"You did that yourself."

"I was being delicate."

Sam decided to let it pass. "Look, man. It's okay. Maybe get a little better and then we can go up after that. You know?"

Gus shook his head. "By then it will be far too late. The

end of the world is upon us. The aliens are nigh."

"Yeah, I mean, if you're being dramatic. But for real. We have no idea how this is going to play out. For all we know, they just do a flyby or something. Or it's meteors and everyone was wrong about … you know. Whatever."

Gus waved this away. "It doesn't matter. The moment is lost. Let me suffer in peace."

"Dude. Seriously. You're being melodramatic. It doesn't have to be the end of the world for you to meet your girlfriend."

"Oh yeah? And what if it actually is the end of the world? What if it's not a flyby? We could be zombie mind slaves by the time this leg's better."

"More like zombie *love* slaves," he said, trying to make Gus laugh, or at least jumpstart a better mood. "I mean. Not that I'm into that. Or anything. Gross. But still."

Gus was staring dead-eyed at the ceiling.

"It's not too late," Sam insisted. "What if we just—"

"It *is* too late. What are we going to do? Go find our two-tire monstrosity back in Wherever, Iowa? Get Ronan to give us a ride? Face it. We're done. We've been relegated, Sam."

"Relegated?"

"Relegated. To the folksy life of the Midwestern farm hand. A new life stretches ahead of us. We will require overalls. And callouses. Do you know how many callouses I've had in my life, Sam?"

"None?"

Gus thrust his hands forward for inspection. "These are the fleshy hands of the intellectual class. These are not farm hands."

"I don't think a farm hand is, like, a literal hand."

"Clearly I have much to learn as I embark upon this rustic endeavor, this new life of plow and of rutabaga."

"You're not going to be a farmer, Gus. We'll pull this out."

It occurred to Sam that the important meeting he had on Monday was starting in two hours. He felt a flash of panic, but it faded surprisingly fast. Once something turned impossible, it became much less urgent.

A sense of weightlessness overtook him. Would he ever see Denton again? Was he was still a data analyst? And if not, what was he?

"Leave me, Sam. I have much to ponder."

"Are you sure?"

"I would be alone."

Sam rose. Some part of him still felt like he was floating. "All right. But I'm telling you, there's more to our story."

"Perhaps, my young friend. Perhaps."

Sam began to walk out.

Gus rolled over in bed, his back to Sam and the room. "Be a good chap and hand me my phone?"

"'Good chap'? Seriously?"

"Just give it."

Sam grabbed Gus's phone and the screen momentarily lit up, displaying the message from Night Fox on the lock screen. In that moment, inspiration struck.

"I'll be running 2x2s on DuelMasters if you want to team up," Gus added carelessly from the bed.

"Uh-huh." Sam pulled out his own phone and snapped a hurried photo of the message. It had Night Fox's address, contact card, everything. This would be perfect. Sam knew exactly how to get Gus out of his funk. And have fun doing it.

And besides, it wasn't like Ronan was the only person with a car.

No, their story was most definitely not over yet.

Chapter Eighteen

Sam walked excitedly back to Nestor's house, his insides bubbling up with the secret thrill of the genius solution coming together in his mind. This could fix everything. He'd have to play his cards right. But it could work. It really could.

And if it did, everything was back to normal. It would take Gus's mind off the big fight. They wouldn't even have any need for Ronan to like them anymore.

Except for all the aliens and the fact that he was stranded in the middle of Nowhere, Minnesota, and at this point he probably didn't have a job to go back to even if he could figure out how.

But still. Baby steps.

He burst into the house to find Nestor at the kitchen table, reading his ancient Bible with a small smile, humming tunelessly to himself.

"Hi. Nestor?"

"Sam," said Nestor, turning to him. "Good to see you. What can I do for you?" The old man smiled expectantly, like he was offering to do anything Sam asked, not just giving a token greeting.

It threw Sam off. Clearly it wasn't actually going to be as easy as just asking, but now he was scrambling to figure out what sort of argument he was supposed to be making to convince the man who seemed already convinced.

"Um…" I was just wondering if you'd mind putting whatever you've got planned today on hold and driving me all the way up across the Canadian border to the house of some person neither of us has ever met so we can bring her down to Lake Peculiar, where I guess she would also have to stay in your house unless we come up with something else, so my other friend can get a kiss from her. If she's willing. And doesn't shoot us on arrival.

Yeah. That would work.

"So … you know how you gave us a ride here to Lake Peculiar? And you've been letting me stay with you and everything? Which is really great of you, by the way, and I'm so, so thankful."

"I do," said Nestor, still grinning. He always looked thrilled. His grin should have been looking creepy by now. Except … it didn't. It wasn't pasted on. Nestor actually looked that happy all the time. Which was weird in its own way, but not creepy. Not exactly.

"Right. Anyway. Any chance you'd be up for doing that … You know. Again? For someone else?"

"There's always a chance." His grin had temporarily melted away as if to show that Nestor seriously considering the request, but it was still there, simmering under the surface.

"Cool. Right. Well, then … could we? Do it for someone else, I mean."

"Absolutely. I love the way you think. Always got to pass it on. That's what keeps it flowing."

"Right. Totally. Totally. Only, the thing is …"

The grin broke out again as Nestor waited to hear where this was going.

"Never mind. I'll figure something else … I mean. Thanks. But that's okay."

"You have not because you ask not."

Sam wasn't sure what that meant. Maybe an old Norwegian proverb. But the man made a good point.

"Okay. True. Well, then …" He swallowed, fighting off the many layers of anxiety and embarrassment wrestling within him. "I'm … I kind of need a ride to go pick up a friend — sort of a friend — and bring her back here. And she may need a place to stay. And she lives in Canada. And she doesn't exactly know that I'm coming. Exactly."

He took another breath while Nestor continued to watch him.

"But she's not too far over the border. I don't think."

Nestor peered at him for a long, pregnant moment, his smile bubbling back. He finally grinned. "Let's do it. We'll head out first thing in the morning."

Chapter Nineteen

It was mid-afternoon by the time the hearse reached the little staff settlement in Quetico Provincial Park at the southern edge of Ontario.

The highways had been bad, but Nestor had an almost magical instinct for finding the best paths through or around mobbed areas. Sam found himself wondering again whether Nestor was actually connected to the aliens somehow, or whether there was some grain of truth to all of Ronan's talk about the Council of Thirty. Maybe Nestor had some kind of secret technology or special access or mystical powers.

Or maybe it was just good instincts.

The guard house at the staff settlement entrance to the park was abandoned, and Sam felt a flush of relief as he punched in the access code Night Fox had sent. That could have been an awkward conversation if he'd had to do it in front of a guard, or needed an expensive day pass, or ... well, who knew, really?

Sam realized just how much he'd assumed someone would figure all this stuff out. He felt a flash of resentment at Gus. If it weren't for Gus, he wouldn't be here in the first place.

To be fair, if Gus had come along, Sam wouldn't have had to worry about any of this. Gus would have blustered his way through. Which would have left Sam worried, but in a secondary sort of way.

He wondered if he took Gus for granted, if all of his friend's nonsense was a good thing.

Then he caught himself. Appreciate Gus, sure. But no need to go crazy.

Nestor was peering at the numbers on the mailboxes. With a small satisfied sound, he turned into a long dirt driveway, driving slowly to keep the long, low hearse from scraping against the uneven surface. He pulled to a stop beside a snug cabin then turned to Sam. "Ready?"

"Not remotely," Sam replied, though he was grinning.

Nestor laughed aloud. "You're starting to get it. You don't find your wings until you jump out of the nest."

"Yeah." Sam swallowed, nervous but also, for once, kind of excited.

"Or someone pushes you out," Nestor added.

Sam groaned. "Don't say that. I'm in the middle of a forest in Canada. Baby steps."

"You got it. Not another word."

"Great. Thanks." Sam started psyching himself up. "All right."

But Nestor had already covered the short distance to the front door in a few long strides. He turned to Sam with his signature grin and waggled his bushy eyebrows.

"No, wait!"

Nestor rang the doorbell. He stepped aside and gestured to the door. "All yours, Romeo."

Sam scrambled to the door, realizing even as he did that he could have just let Nestor handle it.

"I'm not … It's not for me. We're picking her up for—"

The door opened. A woman with gray-white hair looked out, maybe in her seventies, slight and sharp-eyed. "Yes?"

"Um." Sam realized he had no idea where to begin. "Hi. This is kind of weird but—"

"My God," breathed the woman, then, in a whisper. "*Gustavius*?"

"No. I mean, yes. Not quite. But … How do you—"

"Oh, we've been trying whatever we could think of. Night Fox pinged you, yes?"

"Yes, kind of. I'm not … I'm Gustavius's friend. But yes."

"Thank you for coming. I can't believe you made it. Listen, we're in a bit of a—"

"Grandma June?" called a voice from inside the cabin, presumably Night Fox. "Who is that?"

Beyond her, Sam saw a young woman descending the stairs. The older lady, June, gave a little start.

"Oh! Excuse me. Just a moment. Make yourselves comfortable. Excuse us for just a …" She gestured vaguely at the couch, then darted across the room and pulled the young lady around the corner into a little kitchenette.

Sam took an uncertain step in and found himself in a cozy, rather old-fashioned little living room that formed the bulk of the ground floor. It boasted a wood stove, over-stuffed chairs, a couple antique-looking lamps, and, surprisingly, a fairly high-end VR rig.

Nestor stepped in behind him. He looked around, eyes shining, and took a few deep breaths, muttering something barely audible, maybe a thank you.

Sam looked away, feeling suddenly like an intruder, like Nestor belonged right here, in this particular time and place, like the universe had aligned to ensure he would be here to meet June and Night Fox in their cabin in Ontario now, today, and Sam had somehow gotten tacked on as an afterthought. He found himself a little jealous of — whatever it was. Not even confidence, exactly. Just … presence. Like he knew exactly where he was meant to be. Like he was ahead of all his deadlines. Like he was … content.

There was a real chance he'd never been *actually* content for a single moment in his life. Always some little craving, always some little fear.

Then Night Fox and the old lady — her grandma, apparently — came back out of the kitchen, and Sam realized it was time to explain what he was here for, and that that explanation was going to be perhaps the single most nonsensical explanation he had ever given.

Hi, you don't really know me, but I'm friends with your online boyfriend and he couldn't make it so I drove up to Canada to take you down to America so you can give him a kiss. The hearse is waiting outside.

Maybe Nestor could give the explanation. He glanced up hopefully, and found Nestor looking right back at him, cheerful and expectant. That had probably been a bit too much to hope for.

He gave Night Fox a sheepish smile. She was really pretty, too, which didn't help his nerves. Why did Gus have all the luck?

Although now that he looked at her eyes…

With a weird quiver in his belly, Sam realized Night Fox was blind.

"Hi, I'm Sam." He reached out reflexively for a handshake. Then he realized what he was doing and his hand snapped back down to his side. "Um, you don't know me, but—"

Now she was reaching out to shake his hand. For a split

second of confusion he wondered how a blind person knew where to reach, then, as her hand hovered, he realized she didn't. He quickly reached out and gave her a handshake. At the touch of her hand, he knew he was in trouble.

She's Gus's girlfriend, he reminded himself severely.

"Heard all about it," the grandma broke in. "Thank you for coming. I'm June. This is Journey. It's good you two could make it. We've got a bit of a situation."

June reached out to shake hands as well, and Sam realized he was still holding Journey's hand. He let go hurriedly and recovered himself.

"Situation?" asked Sam.

"Yeah, they're kicking us out," said Night Fox. Or Journey, apparently.

"They're evacuating the park," added June. "And if we don't want to end up in a tent city we've got to make some other arrangements by eight a.m. tomorrow."

"That's perfect!" exclaimed Sam. Relief washed over him. "You can come with us. That's what I was here for, anyway. I wanted to take you back to meet Gus. Gustavius. You know."

Journey started to say something, but June cut her off.

"Great. We're looking forward to it."

"We're — I mean, Gus and I — we've kind of hit a situation, too. We're sort of having to make do in Lake Peculiar. That's where Nestor lives. And some other people. Obviously. He's been really a huge help, kind of getting us rides and a place to stay and—"

"I'm sure we can figure something out," said Nestor smoothly. "You ladies need any help packing?"

"This is Nestor, by the way," Sam added.

The ladies shook hands with Nestor.

"Charmed," he said, grinning his goofy grin.

"You an undertaker?" asked June.

"Not that I know of," Nestor shook his head, momentarily confused. Then it clicked. "Oh, the hearse. No. God gave me that a while ago. Sort of a running joke between us, you could say. Third one so far."

June raised her eyebrows at that, and Sam saw Journey's fingers flick out to touch June's. He wondered if maybe that was a blind person's equivalent of sharing a quick glance.

"My friend Thor says it's morbid," Nestor added, "but I say it's a good reminder. And surprisingly roomy. Really, you'd think he'd be into it. He's usually all about dark and sober."

"Thor, god of thunder?" June asked. "Sounds like you've got a whole pantheon going."

Nestor laughed. "No, no. Thor Halvorssen. Old friend. Fishing buddy. Here, look." He whipped out his phone and started flipping through pictures, then showed June. "We caught that one a couple weeks ago. Isn't she a beaut!"

Sam peeked over her shoulder to see a picture of Thor on a lake dock, standing with a dour smile and a fish a foot and a half long. June's head jerked closer. She zoomed in. Her eyes darted to Journey.

"Wow. That's — that sure is a beauty. And that's Thor?"

Nestor nodded.

"Wait 'til you meet him. What do you think, Sam? You think this time we'll convince him to give up a room or two in that big old rattly farmhouse of his?"

"Oh! I don't think we'll need to worry about that until we …" June drifted off, her eyes sharp with a sudden intensity of thought. "Excuse me," she said. "Sorry. Can you just give us another—"

She grabbed Journey then disappeared into the kitchen again.

Sam glanced up at Nestor, who waggled his eyebrows.

"Was that ..." He wondered whether Journey could hear them. He'd heard stuff about blind people developing heightened senses or whatever. He lowered his voice. "Did that seem weird?"

"Sure," said Nestor, seemingly unconcerned. To be fair, he seemed like the sort of guy who probably had far weirder experiences on a fairly regular basis.

June and Journey re-emerged from the kitchen. Journey's face was hard, somewhere between confused and angry. Or maybe lost in concentration.

"Bit of a development," said June crisply. "I'm not going to be able to come the whole way with you. Although I'd appreciate a ride partway, if it's not a bother."

Sam was impressed. He figured it would have taken him twenty or thirty minutes of hemming and hawing, then in the end he still probably wouldn't have managed to get it out. Even if he did, he would have felt way too awkward asking for different help after he'd turned down the rest.

"You know St. Benedict?" June asked.

"Oh, sure," said Nestor. "I used to run a thing there. Practically on our way."

"Great. Thanks."

"I'm staying with you," Journey blurted. "St. Benedict is fine."

Sam's mind began spinning, trying to come up with arguments to convince her to come with strangers to meet a stranger in a town neither she nor they knew instead of staying with her grandmother.

June laid a hand on her shoulder.

"I told you. You need to go with them." She reached up to Journey's cheek. "I'm sorry, babe. I'm going to need to move fast, and I'm not sure where I'll end up."

"Business trip?" Journey asked sardonically.

A wry smile pinched the old woman's lips. "I'll be back as soon as I can manage. You know I wouldn't if—" The smile widened, but Sam sensed she was holding back tears. "You're going to be grand, babe. Just grand. I'll be back with you soon. Okay?"

Journey clutched at herself, then gave a tight nod. "Okay. Let's do this."

Chapter Twenty

Sam sat in the middle of the front bench seat of Nestor's hearse, wedged between Journey on his right and Nestor on his left. The back seat held Journey's bags and an emptiness where June had been. They'd dropped her off almost an hour ago in St. Benedict.

Now Sam was extremely aware of Journey's arm pressing against his and the scent of her shampoo and clean clothes. He couldn't remember the last time he'd been this close to a pretty girl, and he was doing his desperate best to play it cool. He wasn't exactly sure what that meant in practice, so for the time being he was sticking with not saying anything and not making any obviously creepy attempts to maximize the surface area of their bodies pressing against each other.

But he really did want to maximize the surface area of their bodies pressing the other. Not in a creepy way. Only if it was consensual and everything. And she was Gus's girl-friend. It was important to keep that in mind.

But still, it wasn't like he could help being pressed up against her.

He also wasn't sure what to make of her blindness. He didn't mind it, exactly. Not in the sense of finding it unattractive. If anything was mildly intriguing. Although it also seemed like the sort of thing that would cause complications in a romantic relationship.

Not that that was his concern. But he'd need to make Gus aware. He was the wingman, after all.

Besides, it wasn't any use trying for an uncomplicated relationship. He knew better than that. Romance was about showing you cared, and that took effort. Everybody said relationships took work, and he was totally prepared to put it in whatever work was necessary to maintain a healthy romance. Some little part of him, a part that felt manly and noble, even looked forward to the effort. He wanted to win someone over, show her how special she was, do the hard work of maintaining a healthy and vibrant relationship. Not with Journey, obviously. But whenever his turn came.

And, to be fair, he didn't exactly have the clearest picture of what all of that meant in practice, anyway. He hadn't really had a serious girlfriend before. Not as such. He'd been on some dates with people from apps and things and made out a little with a couple girls in college, but all those had disintegrated pretty quickly.

The silence was getting awkward. Not awkward awkward, because technically they had no reason to be saying much of anything to each other. The second it registered on his consciousness he couldn't help but be extremely aware of it and, more and more, feel the pressure of responsibility falling on him to alleviate it.

He sought desperately for something to say. Something that wouldn't be stupid, or creepy, or one of those horrible conversation starters that falls flat three words in.

Have you lived here long?

Yeah, ever since I was a kid.

Oh.

The End.

Or worse, something offensive. *Don't ask about being blind.*

Not that that was offensive, necessarily. In fact, suddenly and nervously he wondered whether thinking it was an offensive topic was actually more offensive than whatever question he would ask. That was just it. He didn't know. It was dangerous and sensitive and personal ground. Probably something you should avoid, like religion and politics.

The silence began to grow unbearable.

He wished Nestor would say something. Sam was used to Gus filling all the dead air in their conversations, and in the short time he'd known Nestor, the enthusiastic old man already seemed likely to fill the same role.

But now the conversational ball had dropped, and Nestor was making no move to pick it up.

Sam looked up at him, trying to will him into understanding. *Wingman time.*

Well, not wingman. He wasn't trying to make a move on Gus's girlfriend. Obviously. But just — friend-wingman time.

But Nestor smiled back at him, apparently as happy in the silence as he was all of the other times. He jabbed a finger in the air, and suddenly Sam remembered.

When that silence comes, break it.

Sam sighed. He let out a little growl, trying to psych himself up. Then, before he could overthink it, he blurted, "So, what do you do?"

"Yes-s-s," purred Nestor.

"What?" Journey seemed surprised at the sudden question, and Sam was already kicking himself. What kind of shallow, clichéd nonsense was that? What did she *do*? For all he knew that was a horribly insensitive thing to ask a blind person. Swing and a catastrophic fail.

Except Journey was answering.

"I'm a botanist with Parks Canada. Mostly focused on trees, but I cover a lot of bases. Some research, a lot of statistical surveys of plant populations, watching growth cycles, tracking disease. That kind of thing. What about you?"

"Me? Oh. Nothing. I mean …" Somehow Sam hadn't expected the question to come back to him. "I'm a data analyst. Little company back in Denton, Iowa. I mostly, um, try to integrate what we've got coming in from a bunch of different systems into a consistent format so we can — you know what? It's incredibly boring. With any luck, the office will get wiped out and I'll never have to talk about this again."

He suddenly realized how morbid that might have sounded. "I mean, with nobody inside, obviously. But it's a really dumb job. It's not what I originally — um, is your job fun to talk about? Or should I ask you about something else?"

She laughed. Sam felt his spirits rising. Maybe not a *catastrophic* fail.

"It's not bad. Pretty fun, actually. Gets a little technical when you get into the details, I guess. But I've been doing it for a few years now, and it's feeling good."

"That's awesome." Sam's mind raced for another conversational gambit. "So . . . what's your favorite tree?"

Journey laughed. "I should totally have an answer locked and loaded for that." She paused, considering it. "Yeah, I can't. It's like picking a favorite kid."

"Fun fact, then?"

"Oh. Sure. Um, aspens. Aspens are cool. Some aspens

have photosynthetic bark. They can make food even before their leaves grow back in the spring."

"That's good," said Nestor appreciatively. "Fed from within. Yeah."

His head started bobbing like he was grooving on a particularly good song. They pulled into a little gas station and Nestor began the tricky procedure of easing the hearse through the clogged parking lot.

"You said you're from Iowa?" Journey asked.

"Well, not originally. Gus — Gustavius — he kind of dragged me out to Iowa after a while. And it's been good. We grew up together out east." He lapsed in silence, then said, "Your grandma seems cool. Very . . . you know. Active."

"Yeah." Journey said flatly.

Sam knew he really had hit a catastrophic fail.

But this time Nestor came to the rescue.

"All right. Snacks on me. Everybody pick something you love. And while we're here, we can rearrange, get you guys a little more space."

"Oh. Yeah," Sam replied.

More space would be good. Great, in fact. She was Gus's girlfriend.

Journey's fingers fluttered to Sam's shoulder in what he was already starting to recognize as her equivalent of a glance.

"Sure," she said, maybe a little reluctantly. "Yeah."

Chapter Twenty-One

By the time the hearse was nearing Lake Peculiar, it was mid-afternoon and the car had settled into sober silence. It seemed Nestor had a strange knack for finding the path with the fewest obstacles, but after hours on the road, it was clear they were driving through a changed world.

Even second-hand through Sam and Nestor's reactions and descriptions, it was harrowing. More than one burned out husk of a vehicle. Car wrecks simply abandoned by the side of the road. And the noises — shouting, mobs in towns, the constant honking of horns on the highways. She'd even heard some distant gunshots.

And Grandma June had left her alone in it.

The best Journey could figure was that the sudden redirect had something to do with "the old days." There were certain parts of her past Grandma June never talked about, but they still cast their shadows.

All Journey knew — well, suspected — was that she'd been some kind of operative, and even that was only speculation. Her mom had talked with her about it a few times once she'd reached a certain age. Just suspicions, mostly.

All of June's so-called "business trips" and friends at the embassy. Her mom was only eight years old when she thought she'd seen June with a gun. Not that you could exactly trust the impressions of an eight-year-old, but still. Something had been going on in the old days.

Journey clenched her teeth and tried to put it out of her mind. Stay put and wait for the rendezvous. Like she was the chick in a goddamn James Bond movie.

And it wasn't as if staying put with strangers in a strange town was a brilliant solution.

She assumed Nestor and Sam had somewhere to put her up for the time being, but she was already working to calculate how long she would have before needing to find another arrangement, or start paying for it, or whatever. Paying meant getting a job — even if Parks Canada managed to maintain payroll, there was no telling what state the banks would be in, and her cash would run out soon enough. That meant finding her way around a whole new town and community. Not that it couldn't be done, but it was going to be a pain.

Which brought her to the problem of Sam. The last thing this situation needed was another layer of complications. She'd keep it professional, transactional, get herself set up and contributing as soon as she could. Or better yet, in her own place. She wasn't sure what he was expecting out of her — after all, he'd come an awfully long way to pick her up — but hopefully she could convince him that it was better to avoid entanglements.

Except she'd have to convince herself first. Much as she hated to admit it, she was enjoying his company more than she expected. There was something vulnerable and sincere about him. The nervousness. The odd little courtesies. Not to mention the fact that he hadn't immediately jumped into all the dumb blind girl questions. They'd spent the first hours of the ride pressed against each other in the front seat, and she was starting to get angry at herself as she realized just how comforting she already found the feel of his arm against hers, just how much a part of her wanted to be pressed up against him again, some little touch of human contact in a world grown too suddenly loud.

"Lake Peculiar," declared Nestor. "Home sweet home."

"You're here now, you betcha," intoned Sam seriously.

In the front seat, Nestor let out a chuckle.

"Town motto," Sam explained, then, to Nestor: "Is it weird how happy I am to be back already? Like that big tree by the church already feels like — you know. An old friend or something."

"That's how it is around here," Nestor said, sounding pleased. "You think you're just passing through, and then it turns out you're home."

Completely unbidden, Journey's dream asserted itself. She could see again, with perfect clarity in her mind's eye, the old stone church encased in blue crystal, the three stark white strangers, the concentric circles of swaying devotees.

An uneasy feeling swirled in her stomach.

"What kind of church?"

"It's the Lutheran Church," said Nestor easily. "Beautiful place. In kind of bad shape these days, but still lovely. Just got a new pastor, young lady named Ellie."

It was fine. Every little town around out here had a church building. It was fine.

But even the swaying of the turning car mapped itself perfectly onto the curve of that street in her mind, and she knew even though it was impossible to know.

"What's across the street? To the side, I mean. Not across from the front door."

"Little bait and tackle shop," said Sam. "A realtor. And some kind of little …"

"Gallery," breathed Journey.

"Yeah. Why do you ask?" Then it hit Sam. "Wait. How did you know that?"

"Great big tree kind of to the left of the church?" asked Journey sadly. "And a park bench with blue slats?"

Sam was silent, and she could practically see the confusion and fear brewing on his face.

"That's a spirit of prophecy," crowed Nestor from the front seat. "You and I are going to have to talk."

Chapter Twenty-Two

Sam had delayed the moment for as long as he could.

He and Nestor had introduced Journey to Pastor Ellie, and after some discussion, Ellie had kindly offered Journey a room in the parsonage. Sam's heart had sunk a little at that — Nestor's house was a couple miles from the heart of town, and Sam had no car — but it was clearly the better option for the blind woman to be able to stay in a central location. Not to mention having a room of her own, instead of whatever hospitable but cobbled-together arrangement Nestor would manage.

Then Sam had taken his time moving her bags up to her room, making sure she knew how they were arranged and she had everything she needed.

But now, at last, the moment had arrived, and it would have been unwingmanly to resist it any further. Sam stood with Journey in the living room. He watched Gus limp down the stairs, making inexpert use of his cane.

"Ah," Gus said brightly, limping over to them. "Dr. Livingston, I presume."

"Journey," Sam said, inexplicably nervous. "This is my

friend Gus. That I was telling you about. Gus, this is Journey."

Gus swept an arm out in an over-the-top bow, then straightened and took Journey's hand as if to kiss it. "Mon cherie. We meet at last."

She yanked away her hand just in time.

"What the—? I'm not anybody's damn cherie. What do you mean at last?"

"Oh, just … you know," Gus backpedaled. "Long ride and whatnot. But we don't have to …"

Journey glowered at him.

"Take some time. Settle in. We'll have plenty of time for us once you're—"

"Listen," Journey snapped. "I don't know what kind of seduction-artist bullshit you think you've got going on here, but that doesn't fly with me. Get it? I've never met you in my life, and you're already—"

"Sorry!" Gus cried, raising his non-cane hand in a conciliatory gesture she couldn't see. "Sorry. You're right. You're totally right. I wasn't thinking. Totally different situation. Just because we had a little … yeah. No. Sometimes the transition period is hard. I haven't had the smoothest ride myself. I'm sorry. I just … you're really pretty, and I …" Her expression had been softening a bit, but at this it hardened. Gus went back into defensive maneuvers. "Right. Sorry. I didn't mean that. I mean, you are. Obviously. But that's not … How about you set the pace. Whenever you're ready."

"Yeah, no shit. In fact, how about I decide whether there's even going to be a pace."

"Right. Sure. No pace."

"Good."

A heavy silence fell, and Sam found himself oddly elated. Probably adrenaline. Finally completing the mission, getting Night Fox and Gus together. And the fight. Lots of adrenaline there, even from watching, probably.

"Is it strange not being able to see what people's faces look like?" Gus blurted. The silence must have been approaching ten seconds. "Like having to touch them with your hands or whatever. To know what they look like."

She turned to him with a sardonic smirk. Sam was struck again by the incredible symmetry and delicacy of her features.

"Is it weird to have to look at someone to tell what expression they're making?"

"What?" Gus asked dumbly.

Smooth, thought Sam.

"Their expressions. How do you tell what expression someone is making?"

"I mean ..." Gus hesitated. "Look at them?"

"Right. And how do you think I do it?"

Sam had to admit it hadn't even occurred to him to wonder. Not by touching people's faces, certainly.

"I listen," said Journey. "You can tell a lot when you pay attention."

"What do you mean? How do you listen to someone's expression?"

"Like this. Close your eyes."

Gus closed his eyes. So did Sam.

"How do you think I'm feeling?" she asked brightly.

Irritated at an idiot, thought Sam.

"Happy," Gus said. Then his voice took on a note of protest. "But that's just because you're being all cheerful the way you talk."

"That counts. People sound cheerful when they're happy. But it's subtler than that. I'm telling you. You can hear it. You just have to learn to pay attention."

"Is it true that blind people get, like, enhanced senses?"

"Is it true that blond boys have trouble with long division?"

"How did you know I was blond?"

Journey reached over and ruffled a hand through his hair. Sam felt a stab of jealousy.

"Enhanced senses." She took her hand back. "I can just *feel* all that blondness seeping into my fingernails."

"Sorry. Excuse us." Sam grabbed Gus by the arm and started dragging him into the adjoining dining area. "Just give us a second."

Gus tried to pull away, and an abbreviated silent argument ensued.

Sam finally managed to get him out of the room.

"Listen," Gus hissed, then shot a glance over his shoulder at Journey, who gave him a little wave. "How does she *do* that?"

"Good intuition, great hearing, and astonishingly good timing," she replied.

Sam realized just how thoroughly he'd failed to get out of earshot. He dragged Gus to the far side of the dining room table and dropped his volume. "Listen. You can't keep asking her stuff like that. It's ... like, offensive."

"I object, sir!" bellowed Gus.

"Shhhh! Listen. Listen. This is what I'm trying to tell you.

Gus dropped his voice. "What? Because she's blind? I don't see color with blind people, okay, Sam? I'm disappointed in you. After all our years together, I never would've pegged you for an ... eye racist."

"I am not an eye racist! Listen, I'm trying to stop you before you embarrass yourself, okay?"

"Now, Sam. You're getting yourself all worked up. Night Fox and I—"

"See? That's another thing. I don't think she wants to

keep up the in-game stuff IRL. It's like … weird. Just use her real name. Treat her like a person. And try not to fixate on the blindness. You know? Like, regular human interaction mode?"

"Certainly, certainly. I understand what you've done here, and I appreciate it. That said, I think you might be just a wee bit out of your league at this point. Now step back and let the big boys play."

"Big boys? You mean you and Journey?"

"No. The big *boy*. And the beautiful woman. And man. Which is me. Not a boy."

"Whatever. Have fun with her. Just don't blame me if things don't go exactly like you're expecting, okay?"

"Oh, Sam. Sam Sam Sam. So much you have yet to learn about the ways of the world."

"Just stop, okay? She's a botanist. Ask her about trees. Plants. Whatever. All right?"

"Ooh! That's perfect. Wingman for life." Gus started rounding the table, headed back to Journey. "All that stuff I said about you being so astonishingly naïve, I couldn't believe you managed to get your pants on? Forget it."

"You didn't say that."

"Oh. Well that's perfect. Because you're not. Your pantedness is without question."

By now they were back with Journey, who gave them an incredulous look. "His pantedness?"

"Yes. Entirely without question. A gentleman and a scholar, this one."

Sam found himself feeling inexplicably happy about how ridiculous Gus was looking in front of Journey.

"Well, anyway. You guys have fun together," Sam said.

"Of course we will. The funniest of fun. Won't we, my dear?"

"Don't call me that," said Journey. "It's like, super demeaning for someone you just met."

"I wouldn't say we've only just met," Gus objected. "Perhaps in the merely physical realm, you might say—"

At her glare, he choked off the rest of that thought. "Right. Right. Sorry." Then he brightened. "But enough of that. Tell me, is it true what I hear that many of the *sightedly otherly abled*" — he gave Sam a pointed look, just to drive home how un-eye-racist he was being — "are endowed with the second sight? I've always found the motif of the blind prophet to be a particularly existential—"

"Look, can we just … Can you not?"

"Not what?" Gus asked, sounding a little affronted. "I was just trying to make conversation. You know, greasing the wheels of what I'm sure will be a beautiful friendship now that we're finally together IRL."

"Look, you want to try to be friends, that's fine. Whatever. As long as you can be cool about it. Although that's not looking great so far. But whatever. Fine. Can we just stop with the what's-it-like-to-be-blind questions? It's like some idiot game show or the lamest interview ever over here."

"Obviously," scoffed Gus. "I wasn't, like, *actually* asking all that. I was just—"

"What do you mean you weren't actually asking? You were just pretending?"

"Yeah. Something like that. You know. Jocularity. Rapport. I wouldn't really expect you to understand, necessarily."

"What, because I'm blind?"

"That's racist!"

Journeys hand flew up as if to slap him, and Gus ducked away with a shrill little shriek.

She lowered her hand and he straightened.

"Wait. How did you even know where to —"

She tossed her head in annoyance and turned away.

"Wait! Come back. I didn't mean it like that."

She turned back. "Mean what?"

"You know. Whatever. All that. I wasn't trying to, you know."

"I don't. Enlighten me."

Gus scoffed. "You don't need me to enlighten you. You're a plenty enlightened woman. Very, you know. Feminist. Unfeminine. Empowered. That's the one. You're all of that. And that's great. I totally support that."

"You support that I'm a feminist?"

"Yeah, totally. Definitely." Gus grasped at the bit that seemed like it had worked. "I love feminists. I think they should be, you know. I think they're great."

"Wow." She put her hands on her hips. "How very modern and liberated of you."

"Liberated! Yeah. That's the one I was trying to think of! Not empowered. I mean, empowered, too. Obviously. If you want that. Or whatever."

She turned away again.

"No! Seriously. Come back. I didn't mean any of that."

"Oh, so you *don't* want me to be empowered and liberated?"

"No, no. Not — you're twisting my words. That's not what I said at all."

"You haven't really said anything. Are you just — what, trying to make me like you? Because I'm going to be honest. So far, you're bombing pretty hard."

"No! I was — I hear you like trees?"

Sam decided it was high time to make an exit. "I was … I'm about to go and …" His brain scrambled for any sort of second half to that sentence. "Help Nestor with something. I think. I'll, uh, catch you guys later. He made his escape with a wave, barely holding back a sudden urge to chuckle. Then he walked briskly through the streets of the small town, past charming houses in some disrepair, their lawns still mostly brown, still recovering from the long Minnesota winter.

He felt a little bad about leaving them behind. But that's how it was sometimes with Gus. Other peoples' words went only so far.

And, much as it felt unwingmannish to admit it, he was realizing that a part of him was eagerly looking forward to the spectacle of Gus bombing out with Journey. It wasn't sabotage or anything. Just … letting nature take its course. Letting Gus's own tendencies play out.

Not that Sam wanted to interfere in their relationship in any way. It was just kind of nice to win for once instead of Gus. And it wasn't a competition or anything, and really he was happy for Gus. It was great that he got what he wanted so much of the time, that he seemed so sure of himself. Certainly Sam felt bad for him, like any good friend should, about the whole situation with Night Fox.

But that didn't change the fact that he was feeling awfully eager to strike up a closer friendship with Journey, and that letting Gus … well, *be himself,* was likely one of the fastest ways to clinch this particular noncompetition in favor of Sam.

"Sam!" called Pastor Ellie from across the lawn. "Want to help us with some setup?"

Lacking any actual destination, Sam had been wandering across the lawn the parsonage shared with the church. Now, rounding a corner, he found himself in the middle of a chaos of fete preparations — a stack of folded tables, disassembled awnings, and bins of decorations and miscellaneous supplies. A few people milled about in a vaguely preparatory way.

"Sure, what do I——"

"Sam!" called Journey's voice from back in the direction of the parsonage.

"Sorry. Just a second."

He scurried back to find her carefully navigating her way down the parsonage's porch steps.

"What the hell is his deal?" she asked. "You said you guys are best friends? How do you stand it?"

"Oh. You know," Sam said, at a bit of a loss. He didn't want to throw his friend under the bus. And, now that he thought about it, he wasn't quite sure how he did stand it. "Practice, I guess?"

She let out a sharp laugh. "Hey, you want to go for a walk or something? I'm going to go nuts if I just have to kick around in my room by myself. And I don't really know anybody else yet. I guess maybe you don't, either."

"No. Yeah. Totally. Um. I was actually just about to help —— They're holding a fete for the church. Like, a fundraiser. I think the roof is leaking. If you want to help? I'd love, I mean, I bet they'd love to have you."

"God, yes." Journey held out an arm. "Take me there."

"Sure." Sam swallowed and took her arm —— just to guide her —— while trying to dim the smile she couldn't even see. "Yes. Totally."

Chapter Twenty-Three

A couple hours later Gus, Sam, Journey, and a few of the interns from Fresh Fire were hard at work setting up for the fete under a looming bank of gray clouds.

Strictly speaking, Sam, Journey, and a few of the interns were hard at work. Gus had borrowed a lawn chair from Pastor Ellie and was reclining under the big oak tree growing on the church grounds.

"You think you can at least fold the programs or something?" Sam asked a little peevishly.

"I told you, I'm supervising." Gus pointed to his leg.

"Yeah, but —"

"I'm disfigured, Sam. Please try to be sensitive."

"Do you mean disabled?"

Gus looked shocked. "That's so racist!"

Sam sighed. "You know what? Never mind. Let's just get this over with. What have we got?"

Gus scanned the list he'd gotten from Pastor Ellie, muttering to himself as he went. "Dunk tank. Tents. Balloons. Streamers. No, this won't do at all."

Sam felt a sinking feeling.

"What do you mean, won't do?"

"It's all so homely. So rustic in its simplicity. We've gotta punch this thing up a little bit."

"We really don't."

"Quiet, Sam. Yours not to reason why. Yours but to do and die."

"You're dying?" asked Journey cheerily, pacing carefully toward them across the grass, the assist murmuring in her ear.

"Probably," sighed Sam.

"I was just telling my associate here that we need to punch this operation up a little. Add some pizzazz. Some wow factor. Some X factor. Some—"

"That's a lot of factors," observed Journey.

"Yes. Exactly. We're going to ten-X this thing by a factor of one million. And in honor of the occasion, I'm thinking alien theme."

"What occasion? It's a fundraiser. For the church." Journey suddenly seemed like she was having a lot less fun with the banter.

"You know," said Gus. "The aliens. I feel a celebration is in order. Good times will be had by all. We will welcome our new alien overlords in style."

"That's not funny," said Journey.

"It doesn't have to be fun. Just… festive. Maybe some grandeur."

"Maybe you could just start by folding the brochures," offered Sam.

"Screw that," snapped Journey. "Give me a real job. I'll start setting up the awnings for the food stands. Where's the stuff?"

"Leaning against the church building, about fifty feet to the left once you get to the wall."

"Thanks." She turned back to Gus with a stern expression. "Not funny."

Sam watched her go a little wistfully. The way she stood up to Gus was a thing of beauty. And her smile. And her angry face. And the way she didn't take any little excuse to get out of folding the brochures.

"See? She's not avoiding work."

"I'm not 'avoiding work.'" Gus made exasperated air quotes. "I told you. I'm supervising. These are heady matters, Sam. You wouldn't understand."

"Fine. Maybe in between supervising you can fold the brochures, anyway. A good leader leads by example, right?"

"A good leader looks the future, Sam. Brochures are thing of the past. You know what's in the future?"

"Aliens?" Sam asked despondently.

"Aliens! The delivery should be here momentarily. Until then, find something to occupy yourself."

"Yeah? What am I supposed doing?"

"How should I know?"

"I thought you were supervising."

"Big picture, Sam. Big picture. I'm not going to micro-manage you. If you can't—"

"You know what? Never mind." Something struck Sam. "And what do you mean, delivery?"

"All in good time, my boy. All in good time."

"CAN YOU BELIEVE HIM?" Sam railed once he got over to where Journey and the interns were starting to put together the awnings.

"He's got a broken leg," said John Mark, one of the interns. "It's cool. We're here to serve."

"It's not broken," corrected Sam a little bitterly. "He

just chipped some bone when he shot himself in the leg like an idiot. Or he's faking it for attention."

"He shot himself?" asked Carl, another intern.

"Yeah. It was a whole thing," said Sam with disgust.

"Just ignore him," Journey said. "He's being an idiot."

Sam's mood lightened considerably. "Yeah, I just get sick of it sometimes. But you're right. He's not a bad guy. Deep down."

"Someone pass me the next piece of this rod?" said Journey.

There was something remarkably refreshing about the way she could ask for help without being helpless about it. And the way she could put together a freaking fair tent without being able to see anything. Sam would have spent ten minutes looking for the instruction manual just in case, and she just … figured it out somehow.

His mind drifted to images of handing her the next segment of the awning leg. Their fingers touching briefly, their hands lingering perhaps a moment longer than necessary.

"Thanks."

"No problem," Carl said to Journey.

"How many of these are we supposed to do?" she asked.

"Five or six, I think."

"Ask the supervisor," muttered Sam.

That brought a laugh from Journey, and Sam smiled. Before long, they settled into an easy rhythm of jokes and conversation. Sam found himself wishing she wasn't already spoken for. But the code of the wingman was unambiguous, and his first loyalty was to Gus.

"All right," he said. "I think this one's all assembled. You guys want to put it up?"

"Sure," said Journey. "Just tell me what to do."

"We grab a corner of it from the top — here." He placed her hands in the right spot. They were firm and smooth and strong and competent. He was sorely tempted to leave his hands on hers for a moment longer than strictly necessary. Maybe two.

But Gus.

He took his position at another corner.

"And then we just walk backward to pull the top of the awning taut."

They executed the maneuver until the awning clicked into place.

Sam looked over to see Journey grinning — too big and beautiful a grin to make any sense of under the circumstances.

"What?" he asked.

She turned to him, and her smile was brilliant.

"Nothing."

Chapter Twenty-Four

The next morning, as Ellie was in her upstairs office in the parsonage, looking out over the lake and praying, a huge dark bulk lowered itself into view above the water. It was at least one hundred feet long, vaguely triangular, with complex attachments sticking out all across its surface.

"Oh, dear God," she breathed.

The thing was flying slower than it ought to have been able to, especially without any obvious wings, and sounds it made were not the whoosh of engines but a strange ringing resonance, like the overtones of a Tibetan prayer bowl, combined with a deep unsettling thrum in her bones and the bones of her house.

And then it stopped, and hung, and quieted.

"Oh, God. Help us," Ellie prayed automatically, her eyes fixed on the impossible object.

It didn't do anything, and it didn't have to do anything. Its mere presence was enough. Too much, in fact. It was overwhelming.

Her brain couldn't register it as anything but a special

effect, her window a pane of glass looking out onto a big movie screen.

It was so still, so rock-solid, hovering several stories above the rippling surface of the lake in the stiff morning wind, and she had the queasy sensation that it was the only fixed point in sight, that it was the real ground and she was huddled against some lump of earth hanging in space.

She peered at it, unable to tear her gaze away. It was impossible to say quite what color it was. The light seemed to fall into it, returning warped into some spectrum that was not quite right, not quite the one she knew, something out of this world.

It occurred to her that every piece of it, every knob and jutting handle, had been made far, far away by intelligences entirely unknown to her. Something had held these objects in its hands or tentacles or with telekinetic powers—

Again her mind rejected the sheer distant foreignness of the object. She swallowed, suddenly on the verge of throwing up. It was utterly disorienting.

Ellie wanted to look away — not just look away away, but to un-know the thing.

She'd been faintly derisive when she'd first seen the reports of the riots in the big cities and the general breakdown of society when the anomalies had first been cited. Nothing had even happened yet, and people were turning insane, in some cases monstrous. There hadn't even been anything to react to yet, and everyone had cranked the dials up to eleven.

But now she understood. Now she wanted to ball herself up in every kind of comforting escape and barrier she could manage and never come out again. She wanted to get away — didn't care where, just far far away, always escaping forever, not from the aliens but from the knowledge that something so alien could exist.

Ellie wanted to lock down a little patch of the world she could control and protect everyone she held dear. She wanted someone to protect her. She wanted a thousand immediate irrational things, and yet, she could have none of them.

Instead, she had the invaders, the intruders, waiting impossibly outside her window, above her lake, come from across the cosmos to shatter her reality.

DORIS KOENIGSDOTTIR SAT in her sitting room working on her knitting, letting the news keep her company like it always did, although it was worse company than usual and was making her cranky.

Her body had woken around four a.m., as it often did at this age, and though it annoyed her, she'd long since learned her body had a mind of its own and was, in many ways, exactly as stubborn as she was. So she'd lit a lonely lamp, microwaved some oatmeal, read her Bible, then resumed her work on the blanket she was trying to finish in time for the upcoming fete. It was a passably pleasant ritual, and one she'd grown accustomed to, but today, the usually sedate Minnesota Public Radio announcers were in rather too much of a tizzy for her taste. Not that it wasn't justified. The aliens, it seemed, had finally arrived.

"… reports of flying spheres continue to pour in from around the world. They appear to number in the hundreds, at least. Rioting and looting continue across the country. Authorities are urging restraint and caution. Seriously, folks. If you're hearing this, just — stay safe. We're all humans, and we've got to band together now more than ever."

"Truly an incredible day, Alex," broke in the lady announcer. "We're getting word that fires continue to rage in Las Vegas, with estimates of the damage to the iconic Las Vegas Strip already running in the hundreds of millions of dollars. No indication as yet that the fires are a result of any alien activity, though reports on the ground are currently patchy at best. Closer to home, spheres have been spotted over St. Cloud, Rochester, Minnetonka, and, of course, St. Paul, with smaller craft also reportedly flying overhead in a wide variety of locations. We'll be getting you more detail as it becomes available. And we're still standing by for a statement from the White House, expected to start any minute. In St. Paul, the governor has declared a state of emergency and will be allocating—"

Doris switched it off with a small sound of disgust. She would have been part of the frenzy in her younger days, she supposed, though it was a toss-up whether she would have been frenzied with excitement or with fear. She pictured a younger version of herself, maybe a beautiful Doris of the sixties, looting a convenience store or scrambling up onto a Volkswagen Bug or beating a rival looter with an overstuffed shopping bag. It could have happened, she supposed, but now her emotions were thin, distant things, and she had trouble mustering much sympathy for the people looting and burning and rioting in the streets.

Of course, it was easy to feel that way in Lake Peculiar. They'd seen their share of disasters, but it was different in a community like this, where everyone knew everyone and most of the houses had been built by the people who lived in them and there was no point in looting supplies because Sven, who owned the Peculiar Market, would likely as not be handing them out in front of the church if things got bad enough, and if you stole something everyone would know whose it was and where it had come from and smile and tut gently until you gave it back just as quietly as you'd taken it, then nobody would have to say anything about it, although everyone would still always know.

No, there would be no mobbing here, and if any of the young ones tried it, she would see to it they cut it out, you betcha.

Chapter Twenty-Five

It had only taken Gus a couple days in Lake Peculiar to pin down the Peculiar Grill House as the town's Place To Be. It seemed like half of the people who came by the parsonage for committee meetings or prayer meetings or closed-door conversations in Pastor Ellie's office were either arriving from the grill house or headed out to it when they left. On his second evening in town, he'd limped the block and a half from the parsonage to the grill house just to see what all the fuss was about.

In eight minutes, he was convinced. Greta, the plumper of the two plump waitresses, had poured him a mug of coffee without even asking and brought him a plate of biscuits "to warm up with while you choose." Most people looked askance at Gus when he consumed caffeine that late at night, not to mention when he carbed up in preparation for a meal. But Greta was a kindred spirit. She understood. And then Mel, the smaller of the two plump waitresses, had slipped him an extra biscuit to help him "get some meat on his bones."

Lily, the skinny waitress, hadn't interacted with him

directly, but she'd smiled from across the room once or twice, and Gus considered that a fine way to make a strong first impression.

So the morning of the arrival, there was no question where Gus would end up. He woke to the sight of an alien scout ship paused in the air over the lake and let out a great whoop. Then he limped outside for a better look. Upstairs for a closer look. Back downstairs to snap a few dozen clips. And then, with a few more whoops for good measure, Gus began limping at top speed toward the Peculiar Grill House, shouting over his shoulder for Sam to join him before realizing Sam was in a different house out on the edge of town. So he kept going, alone.

At moments like this especially, the Peculiar Grill House was the place to be.

He arrived to find it already packed with customers and buzzing with conversation. Greta scurried past with four huge platters loaded down with steak and eggs or generous stacks of pancakes.

"Grab a seat anywhere, sweetie," she said, sounding harried. "You'll have to share a table."

"Oh, sure, sure," he replied, already scouting the area.

"I heard Lily already up and ran off in the middle of the night," confided a lady from a nearby booth. "Mel and Greta sure are doin' their best, though, you betcha."

Gus nodded absently.

"You see the spaceship?" asked one of the woman's companions, rather unnecessarily.

"Scout ship," Gus replied automatically. "Designed for rapid surveillance. In and out. I'd put the threat level at about six out of ten, tops. Nothing to worry about."

He drifted on and then, spotting some familiar faces, made a beeline toward a table of six or eight.

"Pastor," he gushed, shaking the hand of a gangly man

he'd seen around the premises of the Lutheran church. He couldn't quite remember the man's name, but he was pretty sure he was one of the rival pastors Ellie had been currying favor with. "How are you this fine morning? Tom, is it?" he added, shaking hands with one of the pastor's hangers-on, a college-aged kid with floppy hair.

"Todd," said the kid. "Pleasure. Gus, right?"

"Absolutely, absolutely." Gus moved to help himself to an empty chair, only to find that there were none. He turned and called in the general direction of one of the scurrying waitresses. "Can we get another chair over here?"

"Crazy thing, isn't it?" said the pastor, if indeed he was a pastor.

"Fairly routine, fairly routine," Gus said. "Quick scan of the area. Scout ship. You can tell from the pointed nose and the aerodynamic shape. Probably only lightly armed. Just scanning the perimeter. You know. Standard procedure."

"How do you know all this?" Tom asked. Charming, really, the yokel-ish desperation of these people. Ripe for someone to lead them into a new dawn.

"Don't you worry, my good man." Gus gave him a heartening clap on the shoulder. He looked about vaguely for the chair that should have been arriving and wasn't. "We'll have them out of here in no time. Just you wait."

"You know," said the pastor, "if you look at the trumpet judgments in Revelation, I think you can start to see a correlation with the—"

"I'm not familiar with his work," Gus said. "Where is that chair?"

"No, no, you should listen to this," urged one of the other denizens of the table. "Really incredible stuff. Pastor Jonathan" — *That* was it. Jonathan. No doubt one of the lesser, peripheral pastors. — "has studied these passages for years. There's so much to see when you really look."

"Precisely, precisely. Just what I always say myself. Of course it's…" He drifted off, looking around for the chair. "What do you have to do to get some pancakes around here?"

"'Hail and fire mixed with blood,'" said Pastor Jonathan. "That sounds to me like debris burning up on re-entry, oxidizing as it's exposed to the atmosphere. Then it talks about a third of the earth and trees and grass burned up. I think we saw the start of that with Moscow, Vegas, all of that. Seems strangely selective, doesn't it? You'd expect invaders to be entirely peaceful or put on the full scorched earth show of force. But we're seeing something in between. They're burning up just a fraction—"

"Definitely. Definitely." With regret, Gus concluded the chair was not coming. "Keep up the good work, boys. With any luck they'll decide we've got something worth checking out, right? Might even get a chance to meet these guys in person. If that's the term."

"I think if we see one of the motherships falling into the sea next—"

But Gus was moving on.

"I'm just wondering whether we shouldn't consider an evacuation," a mousy man was muttering to his companions one table over.

"Don't be silly," said Gus. "Just a scout ship. Completely routine. And besides, chances are they'll be bringing us a whole panoply of new opportunities. Technologies that boggle the mind. Miracle cures. That sort of thing."

"Who are you?" asked one of the tablemates.

"I'm Gus." Honestly, you'd think these people would

have picked up a thing or two by now. "I'm with Pastor Ellie. Who are you?"

"Sander Block." The man was heavy-set, probably fifties, with thick salt-and-pepper hair. He gave Gus's hand a firm shake.

"Pleasure."

"Barty Olufsen," added the mousy man.

Gus gave him a nod and a handshake as well.

"Mayor Block and I were just discussing whether we might want to consider an evacuation."

"Absolutely. Absolutely. Here's the thing, Barty." Gus did a double take. "Wait. Mayor?"

Block nodded.

"Oh. A pleasure. Really. Glad to meet you, mayor." Gus vaguely cast about for a chair and didn't find one at this table, either. "Anyway. I was just telling Barty here that an evacuation is completely out of the question."

"Well," the mayor began "I don't know that I'd say—"

"Where are you going to go? St. Paul? They'll be clogged to the gills. They'll have more aliens than … than …" Gus looked around, then called toward the kitchen. "Can I get a chair here?"

He turned back to the mayor. "Or what? Some other little town? How's that any better? You'll still be out in the middle of nowhere, but you won't have your houses and supplies. Do you guys even have an evacuation plan? What, some blue binder from the seventies sitting in the back of Helga's filing cabinet?"

"You know Helga?" asked the mayor, nonplussed.

"You have a Helga?" Gus's brow furrowed. "Huh. Lucky guess. Anyway, trust me. You don't want to …" He cast about again. "What's a guy got to do to get some pancakes? Anyway." He waved a hand at the scout ship outside. "Don't worry about — you know."

"That's all well and good," said Barty. "But what if you're wrong? What if they open fire or something? Or … or invade? Or what have you?"

"They're not going to invade!" exclaimed Gus.

"But if they do—"

"I heard they vaporized Moscow," observed the mayor. "These are dangerous beings we're dealing with."

"With all due respect," interjected Gus. "We're not 'dealing with' them at all. Moscow fired first. Anyway. Are you planning to unleash Lake Peculiar's arsenal on the scout ship, Mayor?"

The mayor didn't respond, but he didn't have to.

"I didn't think so."

"Still," said the mayor, trying to regain some sort of control of the conversation. "I believe it would behoove us to form a contingency plan. We don't want to be caught flat-footed if the scout — that is, if the alien vessel tries something."

"Sure, sure. Behoove away. This has been great, but I'm kind of overdue for some pancakes here." He clapped the mayor vaguely on the shoulder and, when Barty reached out for a handshake, returned it automatically before continuing his slow circuit of the Peculiar Grill House, crowing about the scout ship to every table he passed.

LATER THAT AFTERNOON, at Doris's knitting circle, Inna Bergstrom shuddered a little when question of the alien vessel arose.

"Ugh. I just can't stand the thought of them floating up there, looking down on us all and wriggling their little tentacles and what have you. Gives me the quivers."

"They don't have tentacles," said Dotty authoritatively.

"I saw it on the television. There are some that look like great big white men with bald heads and strange eyes, and their pets — or guard dogs, maybe — are slithery black bug-looking things with huge jaws."

"Well, I can't see is that makes it any better," huffed Ingrid. "You want a pack of bald white men and their giant guard bugs looking down on us then?"

"I heard they blew up Moscow," said Kjerstin Florin with some relish. "Flattened it right to the ground."

"Oh, fer — I don't see how it's any of our concern," said Dotty. "What are they going to look at around here, anyhow? They'll scan their scans or what have you, and that's the last we'll hear of it, I imagine. What does an alien life form want with a little old nowhere place like Lake Peculiar? And they certainly won't have any reason to blow us up," she added with a pointed look at Kjerstin.

"Aye, that's what I say." Lottie McNair nodded vigorously, her eyes never drifting from her rapid crocheting. "There's naught they want with the likes of us. Just like everyone else. They'll take a look and move on by."

"They still give me the quivers," muttered Ingrid.

TWENTY-NINE HOURS after the alien vessel appeared, it flew away with as little fanfare or explanation as it had brought upon arrival. Gus immediately began explaining to everyone who would listen that this was a fairly common phenomenon in alien invasions.

"Routine scans. You know. Just checking the perimeter. Nothing to worry about. In and out. No fuss, no muss."

He spoke with enough confidence that a few of the people listening took comfort in his words. Most of the others had their doubts, but Lake Peculiar was not the sort of place where one contradicted the words of confident strangers — not to their faces, at any rate. It was considered inhospitable, and besides, overweening confidence was a characteristic the residents of Lake Peculiar left to outsiders.

Nevertheless, when Gus was proven wrong the following morning, those residents who had doubted him found themselves secretly pleased in a manner which, if expressed openly, would have been rather inhospitable indeed.

Chapter Twenty-Six

Sam sat in the front passenger seat of the hearse as they headed back to Nestor's house.

"One last thing," said Nestor. "We've got to go pop over to see the interns, then we can get you home to bed. Unless they manage to rope you in, after all."

"I'm ..." Sam's mind raced with valid excuses to avoid Ronan. "I don't really—"

"I'm kidding. I just like to check on them now and then. Make sure they've got everything they need. We might have a little prayer meeting. You know. The usual."

"Is that usual?"

Nestor laughed. "Don't worry. It'll be great."

He pulled around to the back of the main building then led the way into the intern house, with Sam dutifully trooping in after him.

A few interns were lounging on the beanbag chairs, chatting, and a couple others were sitting at the long table poring over books and scattered papers.

"God is good!" Nestor announced unprompted as he entered the building.

"All the time," chorused the interns.

"And all the time."

"God is good!"

"Except in occasional cases of genocide and plague," added Ronan's rich and sardonic voice.

Sam hadn't noticed him at first, but it turned out he was also in the lounge area, talking with the interns. What had they been discussing? Part of him would've loved to have been a fly on the wall. Another part of him suspected the confrontation levels in that corner were off the charts, and it was probably for the best he'd found lodgings in a separate part of town.

Nestor wandered over to the long table with the studying students.

Sam, not wanting to intrude on their conversations, stood awkwardly by the front door, wondering what to do with himself.

But Ronan saved him. He hopped up from the armchair where he was holding court and threw an arm around Sam's shoulders.

"Sam. Good to see you. We've got to talk."

"We do?"

Ronan guided him outside, perfectly calm on the surface. The weather was cool and overcast, the lake placid.

Anxiety knotted in the pit of Sam's stomach. They hadn't ever really resolved things since their arrival in Lake Peculiar. All Sam knew was he and Gus were responsible for disabling Ronan's truck and getting him stranded in this little town in the middle of nowhere when it seemed like he had big plans somewhere else.

It's quiet. Too quiet, a voice in Sam's head quoted automatically.

Sam had hoped Ronan just needed him to help carry

something, some kind of simple manual labor. Load up some more tarps for the church or something. Simple non-manual labor would've been even better, but it was probably too much to hope for.

But Ronan kept walking down to the edge of the parking lot, until nothing but a scrubby field separated them from the far side of the lake.

Feeling increasingly nervous, Sam trotted after him.

For a long moment Ronan stood in silence, looking wistfully out over the lake.

In his mind's eye, Sam could still see the triangular vessel — the one Gus kept calling the scout ship — hovering over the water, eerie and impossible. It had hung there, as Douglas Adams had so perfectly put it back when aliens were still fiction, in much the same way that bricks don't.

Sam began to wonder if he was supposed to speak first. Maybe Ronan was expecting an apology, or some kind of offer. He wasn't sure what he had to offer, and some momentary legal instinct gave him pause about apologizing. Maybe an apology was an admission of guilt that Ronan could use against him in a court of law. Maybe that was exactly what Ronan was trying to get out of him. Maybe it was psychological warfare. Maybe—

"I've been doing a lot of thinking, Sam," Ronan said.

Sam felt a momentary relief as his constellation of anxieties dissipated, only to be replaced within moments by another bigger set. His mind cooked up some terrific new worries for him.

I've been thinking, Sam. I think you and Gus owe me a truck.

Or, *I've been thinking, Sam. Maybe I'll only kill one of you.*

"Yeah?" he managed.

"Yeah. And I think we had a bit of a misunderstanding

before. I was acting in the moment. You have to understand. I was very upset."

"Totally. Yeah. We all were. I mean. I wasn't. But you sure seemed like — I was more nervous than, you know…"

"Anyway. I think I kind of tarred you and Gus with the same brush in the heat of the moment. But my beef is mainly with him. He's the one who lied. You're the one he told me the truth. You came clean. That sets you apart in my book."

"Oh." Sam couldn't help but think that would have been nice to know a lot earlier.

But Ronan had already moved on. "Listen. I've been talking to these guys. I'm starting to lay the groundwork for a resistance."

"What kind of—"

"Just listen. There isn't much time."

"Not much time before what?"

Ronan gave him a look and kept talking. "These entities that landed recently. I'm still trying to get a bead on them. They don't clearly align with any of the factions I've delineated so far. I'm pretty sure the Council of Thirty had some inkling they were on the way, but there hasn't even been much chatter beyond that. These guys will be game changers, and I don't think it's going to be in a good way."

"I don't know. Gus was pretty excited about—"

"Gus is an idiot. Listen. We're going to have to mount a resistance, and we might not have much time to do it. We're not exactly working with the cream of the crop here, either. But they're eager to help, they're not going to ask too many questions, they're strong, and they work hard. And that's not nothing."

"You ready?" called Nestor, appearing at the door.

Sam glanced at Ronan.

"Give us a minute," Ronan called back. His voice

dropped. "Here's what I'm going to need from you. Start sounding out the people you run into. See who's going to be on our side. I'm going to need you to be careful about it. I'm still trying to figure out what the affiliations are here. Nestor's clearly connected, but I'm still not sure to what side. You can keep an eye on him for me. See what kind of — Hmm. I don't suppose you know about lexical markers or allegiance tracing or any of that?"

Sam shook his head.

"You might want to start listening to some back episodes of my shows. I'll try to get you a list. But it's gonna be a lot of catch-up." He put a hand to his chin, momentarily lost in thought. "Yeah, we may not have time for that."

Sam felt a rush of relief and an aftershock of guilt. "Maybe I could, like, recruit people? I mean, unless I'd need the — you know. Lexical stuff."

"No, that's good. I like where your head's at. Keep an eye out. I can help you vet likely candidates. There's just one thing in the meantime. And this is more important than any of it right now."

"Yeah?" Sam felt a creeping dread and wondered why exactly he had volunteered to help. Two more minutes, and he might have gotten out of there with no more than a vague commitment to keep an eye out, whatever that meant. Now he was practically part of the conspiracy. Whatever it was.

"I'm pretty sure these things will have some form of paranormal perception or communication. Potentially across great distances. Maybe just close range. It's hard to tell until we've gotten a better chance to observe them. But for the time being, we're going to have to treat them as if they're fully clairvoyant."

"You mean like … psychic?"

"Something like that. The point is, we cannot afford to tip our hand. You get that? This is of critical importance. If they get wind of what we're planning, we'll be done before we even start. We'll be toast. I'm talking survival of the whole town in the balance. So I'm going to need you to scout for like-minded people, but you can't speak openly about what we're doing, what we're planning. Not a word against *them*. If you can keep from even thinking it, so much the better. Understand?"

"But—"

"You heard what happened in Moscow, right?"

"I heard — I heard they flattened it." It felt like a movie, too big to take in.

"Exactly. They fired on one of the motherships. Nukes. Didn't make a dent, and then the entities leveled them. Moscow made too much of a stink, now there's no more Moscow. I don't want that happening here. We'll stand up to the aliens when we're good and ready, but if we make a move before the pieces are in place—"

He slammed a sudden fist into his open hand.

"Bam. Moscow all over again. Until then, not a word against the aliens. You don't have to be all rah-rah about them, but I get the sense that if they get a whiff of resistance, it's gonna be bad news for all of us. You understand?"

"Totally. Sure."

"And you agree?"

"Yeah. I mean, I think so. I mean—"

"You want obliteration or victory, Sam?"

"I mean. You know. Given those options—"

"Exactly. I hope I can trust you on this, Sam. Your friend already screwed me once. I don't like getting screwed, Sam. I don't like people who screw me. I trust I can expect better things from you."

Sam gulped. "Totally." An insistent little doubt nagged at him. "But aren't you …" Sam's eyes darted to the scout ship away over the lake. From this distance it looked like a toy pinned to the sky. He hesitated, trying to figure out how to put it. "I mean. Telling me? Right now? With your words?"

"It's early, and they're far away. And I'm keeping it brief and vague. I don't like it, but we've got to start somewhere. But that's a good point. You've got your eyes open. That's good. That's just the kind of mindset I'm looking for here."

Sam felt a little rush of pride.

"So we're clear?" Ronan asked. "On the surface, we're happy to see them. Until I give the signal, not a word against them. Not a thought. Don't betray hostile intent."

He caught Nestor's eye from across the parking lot and signaled that they were about done. Nestor nodded and began walking over.

"Remember," said Ronan, grabbing Sam's shoulder and pinning him with a piercing stare. "This could be the difference between life and death. Not just for you and me. For the whole town. For everybody."

Chapter Twenty-Seven

Journey was sitting on the front porch thinking when the outcry began. She was *trying* to think about a more permanent solution to the question of where she and June could live, supposing the rendezvous happened. Now that the aliens had landed, the borders were probably closed, and there was no telling if or when they could get back into the park.

She was *actually* thinking about whether Sam would say yes if she asked him to the fete as a date. She had the feeling he wanted to, but he kept getting all awkward anytime it seemed like they were about to have a moment. It was infuriating, in a cute sort of way.

When the outcry started up, it sounded like someone had started an incongruous sports match some distance down the street. A murmur of shouts and conversation began building. There was something off about it. Like a parade without music, or a fight that kept getting bigger and closer, or an unusually organized riot. At this distance, she couldn't quite tell whether the people were scared or excited. She rose from her seat, and that was all the time it took her to understand what was happening.

It had to be the aliens.

By now, enough intermittent TV broadcasts had made it through that she knew the white men in her dream were three of the alien species already coming to be known as the titans. Part of her still refused to accept the dream was real, still tried to write it off as some kind of coincidence or maybe a psionic impulse in her brain getting interpreted into a false vision of disaster to come. But deep down, she knew better, and as the pieces fell into place, she felt terrified despite herself.

With a touch of exasperation, she had a realization — in her head, she was narrating all of this to Sam. But then, why not? He was a good guy, and even if he had a tendency to get weird, she could talk to him. As a friend.

The roar grew closer, and she figured out what was off about it. What she'd taken for the far-off rumble of a shouting crowd was a closer, murmuring horde.

Taken in aggregate, the crowd had a panicky edge. She couldn't make out any individual words, but the tone was urgent, nervous, like everyone was too scared to make a ruckus and had started talking quietly to the person next to them, instead. Except it was dozens of people all talking to their neighbor simultaneously.

Journey had been taking careful steps toward the edge of the porch, feeling for the pillar beside the stairs.

"Steps ahead," said the assist into her ear.

She felt for the banister and began walking down onto the front porch.

Sam should be next door in the church building, she was pretty sure. Nestor had brought him over to help out with something or another.

It seemed to Journey that, for a member of the weird little Pentecostal church at the edge of town, Nestor spent an awful lot of time at the Lutheran Church.

Then again, why not? The building needed all the help it could get, and in a town this small, you probably couldn't afford to build fences instead of bridges.

She made her way out to the sidewalk and turned sharp left. The church building was next door, and her assist was good at guiding her along well-defined paths like sidewalks, but still she walked with deliberate steps, unwilling to trip or crash into an unseen obstacle.

Her dread and urgency grew, the crowd growing closer and louder as she slowly paced nearer to the church, step by step, feeling like she was in a bad dream where if she could just get her legs to move faster the unseen horror couldn't capture her. But she may as well have been walking in drying concrete.

Except it was worse, because there was nothing wrong with her legs. She was just too scared to run. She'd only run twice since turning blind, both times in a wide open spaces she knew well, with June keeping an eye out for her. And still they had been terrifying. Empowering, sure. It was good to prove to herself she could do it. But it was like jumping off a cliff over and over and over with every step.

The crowd was getting closer. Her body shuddered with nerves.

"Stop it," she snapped at herself, but her body wouldn't listen. The hairs on the back of her neck began to tingle, like she could feel the titans breathing on her. Which was ridiculous, of course. They had be a few blocks behind her still.

She walked on, speeding up as much as she dared. The sidewalks were sorely in need of maintenance, and the assist bleated almost constantly in her ear, warning her about small rises and small dips. Not for the first time, she cursed the explosion that had left her blind. It was worth it, of course. Technically. Mathematically. She had saved the lives of children.

But math didn't apply. There was no technically. There was only blindness and uncertainty and the pressing urgency to get away as the aliens approached inexorably behind her.

"Turn left," said her assist. Almost there. With a surge of hope, she turned left toward the church entrance.

"Sam?" she called.

Now the crowd was getting close enough that she could catch snatches of what they were saying.

"Get out of here," said one voice, but the others were less aggressive, more nervous.

"What do they want with us?"

"Where are you going?"

"They're headed toward Vern's Bar!"

"Sam?" she called again, and still her legs would not speed up. The door must be only a couple dozen feet away. She was so close.

But she could feel the aliens approaching behind her. Her skin crawled. There were beings from another world, only a block or two behind her, on these regular asphalt streets in the middle of a little town in Minnesota, of all places. She wished she was home, wished she could see again. Wished her parents were with her. Why couldn't anything be normal anymore? Why couldn't anything be safe?

"Sam?" she cried, desperation edging her voice. Tears threatened, but she fiercely resisted them.

"Step up," said her assist.

Journey trotted up the three small steps and grabbed the thick wooden door by its handle. *Sanctuary! Sanctuary!* cried a reflexive part of her brain.

She pulled open the heavy door and ducked into the musty coolness of the church.

Chapter Twenty-Eight

"Sam?" Journey called again.

As the relief washed over her, she couldn't resist a few huge sobs that wracked their way through her body. Then she pulled herself together.

"Journey?" She heard his voice from around the corner, followed by his running footsteps, and then he was there.

"Sam. Thank God. They're here."

"What? Who's here?"

"The aliens. Titans. They're coming."

"What do you mean? I thought they left."

"Look." She pointed behind herself at the door, unable to go back to it herself.

The door creaked open. For a moment, the hubbub of the crowd outside swelled. They must be very close, going past the building. Everything inside her wanted to cower away, get down into the basement and cover herself up, anything to hide herself from those presences.

"God," breathed Sam behind her.

The door creaked shut. For an irrational moment,

Journey was sure he had dashed out to join the swarm of people being drawn into the aliens' undertow.

But no.

"That's insane," he said. She felt him draw close. "Are you okay?"

She longed for him to hold her, but only so he could tell her it would be all right. *Fantastic,* snapped the voice in her head. *Just a scared little blind girl in a big, bad world. Idiot.*

Journey forced herself to stand up a little straighter, to draw away a little. She looked at where his eyes should be. "Can I tell you something?"

"Yeah, sure. Of course. Totally."

"I've known the aliens are coming"

"Yeah. I mean. The Astral App, right?"

"No. For weeks, Sam. And—"

"But they only got sighted—"

"I know. Just — can I just get this out? Sorry. It's kind of — it's bad."

"Yeah. Sure. Totally."

"Thanks." She hesitated, but this time he didn't interrupt, and after moment to gather herself, she continued. "I've been having these dreams. I mean. I've had these dreams. A few times in my life. When I saw something that was going to happen. Something really bad. They came true. Three different times. I'd have the dream for a few weeks, then the thing would happen."

Journey swallowed. It was a queasy thing to talk about, and half of her was terrified she was convincing Sam she was a nut job, that any chance she had with him would be out the window if she let much more out. But it also felt good. Not just good. Necessary. She had to get it out somehow, to someone, or she would break down.

"Anyway. I've been dreaming about these aliens. I didn't think it was real. I mean, I was hoping it wasn't. It didn't seem like it could be real. Three tall bald man with *really* white skin?"

Another wave of fear and nausea crashed over her. Part of her couldn't accept that the fourth dream was real, couldn't come to terms with whatever threat it would bring into her life, whatever sacrifice it would require of her. Another part had always known. It was like finding out her parents were dead all over again. The small part of her that always expected the other shoe to drop had finally been vindicated while the rest of her was unable to make sense of such a sudden and drastic change in her reality.

"That's …" Sam didn't seem to know what to say.

Not that she blamed him.

Nonsense. Crazy. The most ridiculous thing he'd ever heard.

"That's huge. I mean. Are you sure? I've never heard of anything … you know. I mean, I guess I never thought aliens were real, either. And there's Nestor. But still—"

"I don't know. I'm just telling you what I've seen. What's happened to me. Before. But Sam, I saw three titans in the middle of town. Over and over, every night I saw them. For weeks, long before Astral ever—" She shook her head. Outside the crowd was getting louder. Part of her brain was turning the crowd noise to chanting already.

But that was an illusion. Probably an illusion. It was the shape her brain was trying to impose. It would be a little while before the dream actually came true. But then, how long would it be, really? Did they have a week? Days? Hours?

"What are they like? I mean, did you actually see them doing bad things? Like what kind of stuff are they doing?"

"It was more … creepy. I mean, they didn't blow up the town or anything like that. They didn't even say anything. The people were sitting around them in circles, swaying back and forth. Chanting. There were other people, walking down the street in sync, in a pack, like puppets."

It sounded foolish when she said it out loud like this. People sat in circles all the time. What was wrong with people walking in groups? This was coming out all wrong.

"You have to believe me," she said a little desperately. "It was worse than it sounds. It was scary. Like a — like a cult or something. Like they're being mind controlled."

"It's okay. I believe you." Sam gave her a tentative hug around the shoulders. Then he pulled back, as if unsure about the rules around hugging a blind girl. Or maybe just unsure about hugging a girl.

Journey grabbed him. Felt him flinch away before relaxing into the dangerous comfort. She could feel her walls crumbling, feel herself losing control.

She gave him a quick squeeze then pulled back quickly before she began bawling or shaking or something idiotic like that. The last thing she wanted right now was to be the pathetic blind girl. The forgettable cliché. "Thanks, Sam," she said, a little formally. "I … I just … you know. I needed to tell someone."

"Totally. Totally. So … what do you think we should do? I mean, do you think it's safe to go out and … you know, at least look at them? I've never, I mean. It's kind of, you know. Historic."

"I don't know." She could feel the curiosity tugging at him. Perhaps this was how it started. Maybe they had some kind of miraculous draw on the human psyche. Maybe it was like the old myth of the Gorgon. One look and you're dead meat. Maybe that's why the prophets were always blind in the stories. The only people who couldn't see the magnificent illusion.

But she was being ridiculous. A crowd of people were

looking at the aliens, and they hadn't turned to stone or done anything insane, as far as she could tell.

"Maybe just a peek," she conceded.

"Yeah. Totally."

She heard him walking away from her, then the groan of the old church door. The roar of the crowd grew louder without the door muffling them.

"Wow," breathed Sam.

"What?" she asked, her voice coming out more nervous than she liked.

It took him a moment to answer.

"It's just … there really here. You know? Like, in real life. I feel like I'm in a movie or something. Or, or—"

Again the silence stretched between them. She still couldn't make out any individual words in the crowd. Just an undercurrent of excitement and fear and questions.

She couldn't stand it, Sam's silence and the crowd's excitement and the presence of the aliens pressing in on her from outside, even through the thick stone walls.

"Or what?"

"It sounds weird, but it feels like I forgot I'm in a VR. This kind of thing can't be real. It's always just a movie. You know?"

Journey clutched at herself. She felt very small, very alone. She wished she could get another hug from Sam, just disappear together into the basement under a blanket with a good show on.

Her jaw tightened. And then what? Keep running? Maybe just give in and let the aliens have their way with this town? Abandon the people to their cult? Leave a town full of puppets then move on, knowing she'd always be running, knowing what she'd left behind her when she had the chance to stop it?

And where would she go? A blind girl haunted by

dreams in a world taken over by aliens? No. If she was going to die, she might as well do it fighting the one last battle she'd been given.

That was the first time she had admitted to herself what this was about. At some level she'd been assuming it all along. The reality she had been fighting with, the question she hadn't dared ask, much less answer.

But that was it. Journey would probably die here.

The dreams had always had a cost. Her parents. Her sight. What more did she have to lose? It wasn't an easy question, but it was a simple one.

She shivered, clutched herself a little tighter.

"Sam?"

"Yeah." His voice was still distant, distracted by the sight of the otherworldly visitors. "I just can't get over this. It's so crazy. I mean, they're *actually here.*"

"Sam," she said again, and that was as much as she trusted herself to say. A sob was coming dangerously close to slipping out.

He must've heard it in her voice that time.

She heard the door swing shut, then he was back with her.

"Journey. Are you okay? What's wrong?"

"Nothing. It's — I told you. The dreams." She turned away, afraid that her face would show more than she wanted it to. "Look, do you think we could go somewhere? And talk? I really just …"

She turned back, wishing like hell she could see Sam's face. It felt like everything hinged on how he was looking at her right then, and she was completely in the dark.

"Yeah. Sure," he said. "You want to go to a coffee shop or something?"

"No. Maybe the basement. If we can get down there. I

just — sorry. I'm being an idiot. But I just want as much between me and them as possible right now."

"No. Totally. Sure. Here, let's go. You want me to guide you, or—"

"Yeah." She laid a hand on his shoulder and they began walking. "Thanks."

They were halfway down the first flight of stairs when the door creaked open and the hubbub entered the building. Quick steps and nervous urgent voices filled the outer hall.

Journey flinched, maybe out of some reflexive fear that they weren't supposed to be there, maybe because the aliens' crowd had invaded her sanctuary, but no one seemed concerned with their presence.

Sam kept guiding her down steps and into the cool, musty church basement.

"Here, there's a little Sunday school room or something," he said, leading her to an overstuffed couch in a room that smelled like handmade afghans and ancient books.

Footsteps pounded back and forth overhead, but here alone with Sam, the small room underground felt like a safe at the bottom of the sea, unmoved while the storm raged overhead on the surface.

"So," he said after they had settled themselves. "The dreams. You want to tell me more about that?"

"Yeah. I guess. I mean, it's hard to hear, probably. If you don't want to, that's okay." She turned to him, wishing again that she could see his face.

"No. Totally. It's what I'm here for, right?" She could hear his boyish smile. She found one of her own, small and sad despite herself.

"Thanks." She turned to him again, almost reached up to touch his face. "Really."

"Totally." He sounded nervous, but he was sweet even in his anxiety. So sincere. Journey tried to think of the last time she had encountered someone so completely, genuinely kind.

And so she told him. About being a kid and dreaming about Ziti getting hit by the car, over and over, night after night. About her parents' efforts to help her get over those terrible dreams. About therapy. Hypnosis.

About the day the dream finally came true.

At that she fell silent, remembering.

"What happened?" asked Sam presently.

"He got hit by a car. Exactly like I'd been dreaming. We were playing on the front lawn and his ball bounced too far. He chased it into the street, right in front of a red car. I didn't have time to stop him. It was exactly like I'd seen in the dream, over and over."

She let her hand move fitfully across the couch, hoping he would take it. "The scariest part was when I couldn't wake up. For a few hours, I was convinced I was trapped in the dream. Then I slowly realized I was awake this time and it had happened in real life just like I'd kept seeing in the dream."

"That's terrible."

She nodded. "I was eight."

For a few moments they sat in silence, just being together in the face of the awful memory.

Then she told him about the next dream, years later, of the mudslide hitting Anikotkan. Her efforts to organize a rescue. The government's resistance. Her parents' support.

Above them the chaos of footsteps ebbed and rose, but no one disturbed them in the basement.

She shook her head bitterly.

"Anyway. We managed to evacuate most of the village in time. Whole crew of us. Me, my parents, some people from town. Even a couple members of the park staff, despite being unable to convince anybody up the official chain of command. We saved a lot of people's lives. Children. Whole families. But—"

Her voice broke. It was soothing, being able to just say it all for once. It still hurt like hell, though. Even now, years later, it was all surprisingly fresh.

"My parents didn't make it."

"Didn't — you mean they *died?*" Sam was aghast.

She nodded, and despite her best efforts to stop it, a tear ran down her cheek. She wiped it away quickly, though not as angrily as she usually would have. Somehow it wasn't so bad in front of Sam.

"And a park ranger. Philippe. And it was my fault." She raised a hand to stop the protests she knew were coming. "It wasn't really. My brain knows that. We saved all those lives and noble sacrifice and whatever. But there's still always that voice insisting it's all my fault.

"I think June was the one who convinced them to help, in the end. Part of me still kind of wishes she hadn't. I mean, is that terrible? I know it was a whole village, but it was my parents. You know?"

She fell silent, and Sam didn't answer, which was perfect. A relief, especially after the times with Gus lately, to have someone who didn't feel the need to weigh in on everything.

"But it still feels like I did it to them. Obviously I had to tell someone. Who knows how I'd be feeling right now if I'd kept it to myself and the whole village had gotten wiped out without warning. Especially since there was never any hint that my parents would die. I wouldn't think I had sacrificed a village to save my parents. I would've just … sacrificed a village. Because I didn't want to go to the effort of convincing anybody or to keep from looking crazy. It's easy to tell myself I made the right choice.

"But that's not what really hits me deep down. It's subtler than that. It's like, what weird thing is broken in me that I'm the one who sees these things before they happen? What's wrong with me that I get a dream that's going to kill my parents?"

"Wow." Again, Sam didn't seem to know what to say.

Journey was impressed with his ability to, in response, say nothing. Unlike most people she'd encountered in the world, he seemed able to just absorb the pain and sit with it. He didn't try to explain it away or fix it or distance himself. He just shared the load.

"And then the third time it happened …" She fell silent. Even with someone like Sam, she still couldn't.

After a moment, he prompted her. "Yeah?"

"It was bad. There were kids. I managed to get them out. All of them, I'm pretty sure. The weeks beforehand were torture, though, seeing those kids, over and over …"

Once again she broke off, but this time Journey forced herself to keep going. She was in the middle of a costly confession, and now that she gotten this far, it seemed like a waste to not get out the whole story. At least the important parts.

"I was terrified about what I might lose. The dreams have never told me that. I was still grieving my parents. Still getting used to living with just me and Grandma June. But it was kids. I couldn't ignore it.

"I think, in the end, the only reason I made it was because I figured maybe this time I'd be the one to go. There had been a couple times when I thought about—" She swallowed. She'd never said this out loud. "You know. About sleeping pills or something. But I figured if I was going to go, I should at least save as many of the kids as I could on my way out. And I did. But that's when …"

With a rueful smile, Journey pointed at her eyes.

"Anyway. I've been talking too much. Thanks for listening. And not getting weird about it. I mean, I can't see your face, but at least you didn't say anything to make me feel like an idiot." She smiled again, this time with a desperate little laugh. "I just had to get it out. To someone. Help convince myself I'm not going crazy."

"No. Totally. You're not crazy. I mean …" Sam hesitated. She expected to feel his hand on her shoulder — part of her wanted his hand on her cheek — but the moment passed and he kept talking. "I can't even imagine what that's been like. What this must be like."

"That's it. I just need someone on my side. Someone to understand. You know? Gus is all excited about these strangers, and I don't know what the town is going to do, but I just know—" Some reflex spun her around so she could try and look into his eyes, some part of her body that still wasn't used to being blind even after more than a year. "They're bad, Sam. I'm scared all the time. I can feel them pressing on me, even through all this solid stone."

"Pressing on you?"

"I don't know. I finally thought I could write this one off. I figured it was my brain finding a new way to make a stress dream or something. The rest of them were so realistic, and this one was so bizarre, so impossible. Except now it's all happening. I can tell you exactly what those three strangers look like even though I'm blind. I can tell you there's a blue park bench out front with flaking paint. It's happening, Sam. And it's going to be bad. Really bad."

"Totally. Totally. Um. What can I do? I mean, is there anything we can …"

She didn't blame him for letting it hang. Journey

wondered if some part of Sam was starting to wonder what he would lose if he let himself get sucked into her vortex. And it was a legitimate question. She hesitated. Maybe it would be better not to involve him. To protect him.

Maybe there was some way she could stop the strangers. And maybe there had been a way for her to save the village on her own. Could be that was why she got the dreams. Then perhaps her parents—

The idea brought a fresh wave of pain, but she tucked it away for later and answered Sam's question. "I'm not sure. I'll … I'll let you know if I need anything."

"Sure. Totally. Just … you know. Let me know."

She nodded, not trusting her voice. Tears threatened again, at the idea of putting Sam in harm's way, and at the weight of the burden of having to face it all without him. Or anyone.

"It might not be so bad. The dreams just show what's going to happen, right? They don't guarantee it's going to be a bad thing. Right?"

She fought to control herself, managed a small smile. "Yeah. Exactly. We'll wait and see."

Above them, footsteps hurried back and forth accompanied by indistinct voices.

Chapter Twenty-Nine

Later, once the hubbub had died down, Gus led Sam and Journey across the church lawn, impatient for first contact.

"You hear first thing when they arrived they tried to walk into a bar?" Gus let out a jittery little laugh, his words tumbling out too quickly. "What is this, some kind of joke?"

The three tall white alien men — if man was the proper term — were still standing at the base of the church steeple, back to back to back, positioned to see most of the town from their combined viewpoints.

As far as Sam knew, they hadn't moved or spoken since they took up their positions. After that uncannily calm walk in from the edge of town, with no obvious point of origin and apparently a very clear destination, they'd just … stood.

Watching, maybe. Or listening. Or neither.

It was hard to tell whether they were even waiting. The term felt somehow irrelevant to them. Meditating might have been closer, but who knew what went on in an alien mind.

Now he and Gus and Journey were approaching the beings, despite Journey's strenuous objections and against Sam's better instincts. But Gus had insisted, aggressively eager to finally meet a real live alien, and Journey seemed to feel a need to protect him or something, and Sam — well, to be honest, his years-old instinct of giving in to Gus after token resistance had kicked in full bore.

Plus, he had to admit he was curious.

Now the three of them walked across the grass toward what could have been muscular marble statues, except for the slight movements of their arms, the minuscule bodily adjustments that somehow made them seem even more alien, not less, like humanoid trees swaying slightly in the wind. Any human standing that still for that long would have made a point of suppressing those little movements. No human would stand so frozen without it being, at some level, a show. But these aliens weren't trying to prove how long they could stand still, or how still they could stand. They were just … doing whatever they were doing.

Beside him, Journey was swearing under her breath as they walked across the grass.

Sam was growing increasingly nervous. There was something uncanny about being twenty yards away from a body that had been on another world.

Then fifteen feet. Then twelve.

He instinctively reached for Journey's hand and caught himself just in time.

Up ahead, Gus charged forward, oblivious of their anxieties.

He bounded across the lawn so eagerly, Sam felt an almost physical tension between the need to stay close to Gus and the need to hang back from the aliens. Then Gus reached them and — Sam had to blink a couple of times to make sure he was actually seeing it.

Gus was shaking hands with the aliens.

"Welcome, welcome," he boomed, grinning from ear to ear.

Sam half expected his hand to disintegrate like matter touching antimatter, or the alien to suddenly grab Gus and start whapping him back and forth overhead like in a cartoon or — or at least crush his hand in a mighty other-worldly grip.

But none of that happened. Gus gave the alien's hand a few hearty pumps. The alien did not appear to resist. It didn't exactly return the handshake, which made for what looked like an unusually heavy handshake for Gus. But after a couple pumps it seemed to catch on and mimic Gus's action with powerful, deliberate movements.

"So good to have you," said Gus, moving onto the next alien, who responded in almost exactly the same way. "A real pleasure. Believe me. A real pleasure."

For all the world, he seemed like a small-time politician glad-handing a group of powerful business leaders visiting from out of town.

"Idiot," muttered Journey. Not dismissively, but like she was scared to the edge of tears and covering it fiercely.

"You guys getting in on this or what?" called Gus.

Sam took a half-step forward as Journey snapped, "No! Come on, Gus. We've got to get out of here."

"It's fine! I have established first contact. They come in peace. Look."

Gus threw an arm around the one that was looking in Journey and Sam's direction. Not over his shoulders — it was too tall for that — but a sort of awkward half-hug around the midriff. Like he was posing for a photo or something.

Idiot.

"You see? Totally docile. This is—"

Gus's eyes went wide, and a flush arose in his cheeks. For an irrational moment, Sam was sure he was about to explode or catch fire from within, or maybe fall over dead with ecstasy.

"Oh, man. These guys are the real deal. Sam, you've got to get in on this."

"No," snapped Journey again, just as Sam took a step or two in his direction. "Gus. I'm serious. Get over here this instant."

"Wow!" Gus's eyes turned up to some distant point on the horizon.

"Sam. Help me get him."

Journey laid a hand lightly on his arm for guidance, then they covered the last few steps together.

Now Gus's jaw was slack and his face was serious, wide-eyed, like he was seeing the mysteries of the universe revealed, or maybe his approaching doom.

"Come. *On.*" Journey felt for Gus, grabbed his shoulder, yanked hard. Sam, trying to be helpful, grabbed Gus's hand and pulled him over to break contact with the alien.

Gus came to himself. "Dude! You have got to try that!"

"No, Gus," said Journey in a tight voice. "We have to get out of here."

"What did they do?" asked Sam. "What was it like?"

"I know what we have to do," said Gus in a faintly awed voice. "A welcome ritual. They showed me. I know what they need. And we're the only ones who can give it to them."

There was a new lightness about him, a new calmness. Like he had been enlightened. He didn't raise any real resistance as Sam and Journey led him away from the aliens, just looked around like he'd discovered a new color.

"How do you know it's not a trick?" asked Journey.

"What did they offer?" asked Sam at the same time.

"It doesn't matter what they offered," Journey snapped. "How do you know we can trust them? How do we even know you understood them right?"

"It wasn't like that. You don't understand. You just have to see for yourself." He paused, still smiling, and laid his hands on their shoulders. "Go. Touch them. You'll see."

Sam glanced at Journey. "Gus? Buddy? You're kind of freaking me out here. What is it you think they said to you? Because they weren't talking. And you're kind of acting all weird now."

Gus chuckled. "Oh, Sam. Trust me. No need to worry your little head about that. This is going to be great."

Already the ethereal daze seemed to be lifting from Gus, his usual brisk manner returning.

"All right. This is what we've got to do. The fete will be perfect. Everybody will be coming here, anyway. It'll be great. The aliens told me what they need."

"What they need for what?" cried Journey. "Gus, what did you offer them? What do they want?"

"Relax! It's nothing bad. They want to help us. They showed me — well, it's hard to put into words. But it's really, really good." Again that distant smile began to claim his face. Relaxed, almost goofy.

"Yeah? How do you know they weren't just manipulating the pleasure centers in your brain or something? What if this is bait? What if it was some kind of drug or something?"

"You say pleasure centers like it's a bad thing," Gus protested.

"It sure as hell doesn't have to be good," Journey shot back. "What do you think heroin does?"

"They did not give me heroin," scoffed Gus. "Anyway. We're getting off the subject. I know what we're going to do tomorrow at the fete. They need voluntary participation, that's part of it."

"Willing sacrifices?" Journey challenged him.

"Nobody said anything about a sacrifice! Geez. You're blowing this out of proportion. I'm telling you. This could be the dawn of the new era. Peace and enlightenment. Brotherhood among nations. Lions and lambs. All that."

"So we're supposed to just bend over and let them do whatever they want to us?

Gus chuckled. "Your mom——"

"Gus," Sam warned.

"Right. Sorry. Inappropriate. I'm telling you. New Gus will be totally beyond that kind of thing. New all of us will."

"I don't want new me. I like me the way I am. And I especially don't want them interfering with my brain in some sketchy unknown new way for unfathomable purposes. Sam, back me up."

"Oh. Yeah." Sam's mind flicked back to his conversation with Ronan. *Until I give the signal, not a word against them. Not a thought.*

He saw again Ronan's fist slamming into his hand.

Would the aliens actually crush them if they sensed resistance? He glanced nervously over his shoulder to the three figures standing impassively perhaps a dozen yards away. Were they listening? Were they watching his mind?

This could be the difference between life and death. Not just for you and me. For the whole town. For everybody.

"Could they read your mind?" he asked Gus, partly out of curiosity, partly trying to change the subject.

"They didn't have to," Gus said a little dreamily. "They *know*, man. They were telling me stuff. *Everything*. Like, galaxy mind. Like, you wouldn't even believe it."

"So, they can read minds, then?" Sam insisted. "Or, like, have psychic connection of some sort, at least?"

"They are psionic beings of a higher order. These are no crude psychic phenomena, Sam. These are not the mystical mumblings of a lady in a shawl or a turbaned foreign gentleman with a curl in his waxed goatee."

"Fine. Psionic. Whatever." Sam glanced again over his shoulder. "I just mean, will they ..." He tried to give Journey a meaningful glance, but obviously she couldn't see it. Could he whisper a warning in her ear? How good was the aliens' hearing? And did they know English?

But Gus was already going on without him.

"I saw a vista, Sam. A panorama, unfolding before my mind's eye—"

"I *don't* want to hear it," said Journey.

"Trust me," Gus insisted, "you really do. It's going to be unlike anything else."

"Can we maybe walk and talk?" Sam asked, feeling desperate. He didn't know whether moving away from the aliens would reduce their ability to tell what he was saying or thinking, but it sure couldn't hurt. He glanced quickly at Journey, then at Gus, trying to weigh their motivations and keep everything aligned. "I just feel like it's kind of rude. You know? Talking about them right in front of them like they're not here? It's like ... talking behind their backs. Come on, Gus."

He laid a few fingers lightly on Journey's shoulder for guidance then began walking away.

Gus didn't follow. Journey turned back.

Sam groaned.

"We're supposed to do a welcoming ceremony," Gus continued as if Sam hadn't spoken. "You know. Let them in. Like, show that we accept their tutelage. We come in peace. Take me to your leader. All of that."

"Like hell we accept their tutelage." Journey slashed a hand through the air. "They do not come in peace. We do not want any of our people anywhere near them. If there's a safe way to get them out of here, we do it. Otherwise, we isolate. Evacuate if we have to. Trust me on this, Gus. They're bad news. Don't let them suck you in with some weird mind trick."

"It's not a mind trick. These aren't Jedi. Please, Journey. The have secrets to share with us. Secrets of great power. Ecological advancements like you can't imagine. It's about the mind. And the body. The connectedness of all things. The true source of pleasure." His voice had been grandiose, almost theatrical, but now it broke into his regular way of speaking. He wasn't saying what he thought sounded awesome. He was saying what he actually thought. "Seriously. It's like the coolest thing ever. Watch. They already gave me a trick."

He reached out a hand and laid it on her forehead.

Journey flinched away as if it was red-hot. "Don't touch me! Get the hell away from me, Gus."

"God. I didn't even do anything. Here, look."

He turned to Sam and laid a hand on his forehead. Sam flinched but hesitated instead of pulling away like Journey had. The hesitation was enough. A small pulse seemed to emanate from Gus's hand, like a light magnetic field or something, then Sam felt a weak but refreshing sensation pass through him, somewhere between the emotion of relief and the feeling of his sinuses suddenly clearing.

"Wow. What was that? Did you … what did you do to me?"

"What did he do to you? Sam?" Panic tinged her voice, and Sam rushed to reassure her.

"It's fine. He didn't do anything. I mean, nothing bad. It was just, like, a little refreshing. What was that, Gus?"

"See?" Gus puffed up with eager pride. He practically glowed. "Don't worry. It's nothing permanent. It's a nice little splash. It's refreshing. They gave it to me as a gift. You know, to show they're friendly. Shows what kind of stuff they can do."

"How the hell do you know it's not permanent? How do you know anything? What if they infected your brain with some psychic virus and now you've infected Sam?"

"Please. Journey. Calm down. You're starting to embarrass yourself."

"I'm not embarrassing shit. Am I the only sane person left here? Sam, what did he do to you?"

"Nothing. I mean. It just kind of felt nice for a second. I feel a little lighter. I think it's already going away," Sam added in an attempt to reassure her. It might have been going away. It was hard to tell. It wasn't like much had happened in the first place. He hoped.

Although now that he thought about it, Journey was right. What if Gus *had* infected him with a psionic virus? It was exactly what you'd expect from Gus.

"Nothing? You call this nothing? Don't you get it, Sam? This is exactly what I was telling you about. This is how it starts. Do you think they're going to gather a bunch of zoned out mind puppets by doing things that feel bad? Don't you get how dangerous this is?"

A sinking dread began to envelop him. "Totally. Totally." Sam eyed the aliens nervously. He wondered what happened when they wiped a community off the map. Was there some kind of build up or warning? Or was it just—

BAM!

Once again he saw Ronan's fist slamming into his hand.

"Back me up, Sam," Journey pleaded again. "We've got to block this area off. Keep people away."

"No, it's fine," Gus said. "Look. Here's what they told me. They want everyone to allow them—"

Journey looked horrified.

"They want everyone who's *willing* to come and and make the same kind of gesture I made. A handshake, I guess. That's all. They said they'll bestow a gift. I was thinking we could work it into the fete. Especially since they're standing in the middle of it."

"No!" Journey cried out. "There's no way we're doing that. In fact, we should probably cancel the fete. Sam. Are you hearing this?"

"Yes. Totally. Totally." Again his eyes darted to the aliens standing like marble white statues.

"Then could you say something?"

"Yeah. Totally. It's just …" He thought of her sitting on the couch beside him in the basement, unbearably close, revealing her secrets. He thought of Ronan and his warning.

And sure, she'd had some dreams that hinted at some terrible things. But really, when you thought about it, all Journey had said this latest one showed was people acting weird. It didn't have to be bad. Maybe it was some kind of new ecstatic experience the aliens would teach people about. Or some kind of transitional phase. Integrating intelligent civilizations was bound to have hiccups, right?

And if Ronan was right, resisting the aliens was dangerous. It could endanger the whole town, maybe more. Was it really worth it just to save one person's feelings? Even Journey's?

He eyed the three towering figures uneasily.

Everything is fine, he thought, doing his best to enunciate.

"Maybe we could let people decide for themselves. Or

whatever. Like, it might not be that bad. For now." He tried desperately to signal his intentions. Even with Gus standing there. Even with the aliens. "It might be a bad idea if we're too obvious one way or the other. Right off the bat. With Moscow and everything."

"Moscow? What the hell are you talking about? They blew Moscow off the face of the earth."

"Yeah. Totally. That's kind of ..." He realized that from her perspective, he was making the opposite point and gave it up.

"Sam is making a lot of sense," Gus said. "Let's let the people decide. Nobody is forcing anything. It's an opportunity. We'll give them the chance to take what the aliens are giving, and if it turns out it's not as good as I'm thinking, we'll adjust for it later."

"We can't adjust once we've let them into the minds of half the people in this town," Journey insisted, seeming near tears. "Sam. Please?"

Her look of betrayal was heartbreaking.

Sam did his best to stay firm and chose his words carefully. "I think it would be a bad idea to signal we don't want to cooperate with the aliens."

"But we *don't* want to cooperate with them," Journey insisted, even nearer to angry tears.

"Shhh," Sam said reflexively, then realized how that would come across to anyone who didn't realize the imminent threat of the aliens overhearing. "I mean. Sorry. I didn't mean to shush you. But can we not talk about this right now? I think we should just go with what Gus said. For now. And we can figure it out later. We should talk. For sure. In private. Is that okay?"

Journey was already turning, muttering instructions to her assist and walking away with the quick, surgical strides that were the fastest she could manage to flee unassisted in an unfamiliar setting.

"Well," said Gus, looking around with a satisfied air. "I think that went about as well as could be expected under the circumstances."

Sam shot him a look.

"Oh, don't worry about Journey," said Gus with supreme confidence. "She'll come around. I'm sure of it."

He smiled a beatific smile.

"Everyone will. You'll see."

Chapter Thirty

The moment Journey returned to her room in Pastor Ellie's house, she began violently packing the few possessions she'd pulled out of her suitcase so far. The threat of tears stung her eyes, and after a few minutes of holding back, of transmuting the fear and pain into rage, she gave in, still trying to pack through the sobs. The thousand little frustrations of being blind in a strange house plagued her as she packed, making everything worse until she almost give up and left the suitcase behind or just took whatever happened to be in it already.

It was time to go. If idiot Gus and his idiot pawn of a sidekick Sam were going to be that obtuse — no, that willfully, malignantly stupid about the strangers — she was done with them. For a brief moment, she considered trying to convince Pastor Ellie to cancel the fete, maybe to organize an evacuation. But she knew in her heart it would never fly.

This was the kind of town where people spent eighty years without ever going beyond three counties. The sort of place where you stayed in the root cellar while another tornado flattened your house again, then got out and rebuilt and kept going. And besides, where would they go? Lake Peculiar only had three of the strangers, and they were just standing there. It wasn't as if downtown St. Paul was going to be in better shape right now.

No, this ship was likely to go down with all hands. Ellie was the closest they had to a captain, and she was certainly the type to go down with the ship on principle. They'd be gathered in the crumbling sanctuary of that damn Lutheran Church while it fell to pieces around them, singing hymns at a curtain closed on the world. Hell, half of them had probably somehow formed the idea that this was the way things were supposed to go. The apocalypse at hand. Jesus sure to arrive any minute now. And she certainly couldn't think of a better set up for Armageddon.

No, the best option was to distance herself. Maybe she was the curse. Maybe if she'd stayed away from Anikotkan, the mudslide never would have happened. Maybe these prophecies were self-fulfilling. A dark laugh escaped her at the irony of the idea she'd lost her parents and her sight only to bring doom on a mountain village, just to put all those kids in danger—

She stopped herself. That was a sure path to a depressive tailspin. Still, if her premonitions were somehow causally linked to the disasters, getting away might be the one chance this town had. If it was going to happen with or without her, there wasn't much left she could do to save them as long as they insisted on walking into the mouth of the trap. If even Sam, even after everything she told him

—

No. Not going there either. With a roar of frustration, she slammed the suitcase shut. It was time to go.

"Get me a car," she told her assist.

"I'm sorry. There are no cars currently available in this area."

It had been a long shot. There probably weren't many public cars in Lake Peculiar in the first place, certainly none that would be available now. She'd have to do it the hard way.

"Fine. Where's the bus stop?"

"The nearest bus stop is 2.2 miles from here. Would you like me to give you directions?"

"Sure." It was going to be a long walk, but she had nowhere better to be. At least she wouldn't have any extra difficulty walking in the dark.

"Great. Would you like me to buy your ticket?"

"Yeah. When does the next bus come through?"

"Two p.m. the day after tomorrow," chirped the assist.

"Damn it!"

"Anything I can help with?" it asked, picking up on her subtle cues.

"Yeah. You know how to make a boy less of an idiot?"

Unexpectedly, that was what set her off again. She found the edge of the bed, sat down, then laid back, sobbing. The damned darkness. She couldn't even properly fling herself onto the bed for a good dramatic cry.

As soon as the crying began, an overwhelming sense of betrayal swept over her.

She hadn't been willing to admit to herself until that moment just how much Sam actually meant to her. After weeks of fear and disorientation from the dream, in this unfamiliar town full of utterly unknown people, in the terrifying momentum of helplessly watching the impossible doom she'd predicted unfolding before her step by step, Sam had already become the one thing she could rely on.

Except, it turned out, she couldn't.

The sun continued setting as Journey lay on the bed, sobbing and sobbing as everything she'd shoved inside finally forced its way back out. The nightfall made no difference to her.

Journey was already alone in the dark.

Chapter Thirty-One

Idiot!

Sam couldn't believe himself. He paced through the darkening streets, seething with rage and frustration. He knew he was weak. He'd never really been able to stand up to anybody. But this? This was a new low.

He couldn't escape Journey's crestfallen expression. The way she'd spun away to hide her tears was awful enough. But somehow it was the moment right before that Sam couldn't shake. The moment she shattered inside. And he was the one who had done it to her.

All because of stupid Ronan's advice.

No. That was a lie, and if he was going to be a despicable idiot, at least he could be honest about it. Ronan's advice had given him the excuse he needed, but really it was because he couldn't stand up to Gus. Not even once. Not even for the girl he was starting to realize he—

His brain pulled reflexively away from that thought — a little too soon for *that* — and he hated himself even more for it. Whatever happened to the old courageous love in all the stories? When had knights and heroes given way to pudgy idiot software developers stuck in the middle of nowhere?

Idiot, the voice in his head snapped again, and he walked on into the night.

Chapter Thirty-Two

The emergency session of the Planning Committee for the First Lutheran Church of Lake Peculiar Fundraising Fete had assembled in Pastor Ellie's living room, clustered around a plate of cookies and a pot of coffee. Outside, the wind whipped through the night, preparing tomorrow's storm.

Barty and Pastor Jonathan and a couple parishioners who had volunteered for the committee were there. Dotty and Doris hadn't been able to make it on such short notice, with the night already darkening and the storm beginning to gather.

Not that Ellie really minded that. Uncharitable, but any planning meeting where she had a voice and they did not felt like an advantage she should take.

"Ah, the gang's all here," said Gus, limping in from the kitchen with a plate he'd made for himself. A sandwich and two little bags of chips. With a bit of difficulty, Ellie suppressed a touch of resentment. She'd just served him dinner an hour ago. "What are you all up to this fine, albeit ominous, evening?"

"Just trying to figure out whether we can go ahead with the fete with these aliens standing right in the middle of the space," Ellie replied. "It's hard to say exactly what we can expect from them. I don't want to endanger people or anything, but on the other hand—"

"I read you loud and clear," said Gus, squeezing an extra chair into the circle, "and I'd be happy to weigh in. After all, I think it's pretty clear I'm the best qualified person around here to talk about the aliens and their intentions. Ooh, coffee." He helped himself to a mug. "Don't mind if I do."

"What makes you qualified to talk about the aliens?" asked Barty.

"Easy enough. I met them. A little bit earlier." He took a slurp of coffee. "Ah, that's the stuff." Then he began wrestling with a bag of chips. "And let me tell you, it was a revolutionary experience. I think we're on the cusp of greatness here."

Pastor Jonathan leaned forward. He was a lanky man, and especially in these gatherings around coffee tables, he seemed to be all elbows and knees. "What makes you say that?

"What I saw. When I shook hands with them."

"Wait, wait. You touched them?" asked Ellie. "Isn't that incredibly dangerous?"

"Apparently not," said Gus.

"Look," broke in one of the parishioners, a no-nonsense middle-aged woman named Luanne. "You seem like you came out of it okay, and that's great, but I think it's irresponsible to expose a whole town full of people to a completely unknown alien presence. What if they're radioactive? What if they're …" She hesitated, likely trying come up with something. "Who knows what? Poisonous. Or … or incompatible with humanity somehow. You might not even see the effects right away. In fact, I kind of wonder whether we shouldn't be quarantining this young man for observation, just in case."

Gus gave a robust chuckle. "Well, I think that would be taking it a little far."

It was really kind of impressive how he was able to make everything about himself just by wandering into the room and taking a seat. Ellie felt a grudging envy at the mindless ease with which she assumed he knew best and dominated every conversation.

Part of her felt an urge to take a leaf out of Gus's book. Maybe if she didn't worry so much about how everybody was going to react to the young and pretty new lady pastor, they wouldn't. Maybe all she needed was some bullheaded swagger.

Gus had been rambling on the little, and she turned her attention back to what he was saying.

"—really eye-opening, you know? Mind-broadening. Enlightening, you might say. I think in a way, it was a religious experience. You know what I'm talking about, don't you, Pastor Ellie?"

"I'm not sure I do," she said dryly. "Although I'm glad to see you seem to be in such good spirits after your experience with them."

Pastor Jonathan piped up, his coffee wobbling slightly on his knees. "I'm just not sure it's a good idea going ahead with the event with them standing right there in the middle of everything. Who knows what they'll do? Besides. It's unsettling. It'll put a damper on the whole thing."

"I get that, Jonathan," said Ellie. "But there are other factors to consider, as well." It felt mercenary to say it, so Ellie didn't. Not out loud. But the truth was, this was their last chance at fundraising.

"What other factors? Are we really going to endanger—"

"Pastor, pastor," broke in Gus. "Nobody's talking about danger."

That was, in fact, exactly what everybody else in the room was talking about.

He continued. "In fact, I think we're being a little short-sighted about the opportunity here. Let's face it. This town is crumbling. We need outside help. And how much more outside can you get?"

"But that's just it," said Barty. "I mean, I'm all for getting the money we need for the church building. Me more than anyone, right?" He gave a nervous little chuckle, then turned back to Gus. "But what if they, you know, do something?"

"Marty, is it?" Gus smiled. "I'm sure they *will* do something. In fact, I hope for it. I'm telling you. What I saw when they spoke with me — it was a glimmer of what they're capable of. And it was *wondrous*. I say we open our doors, welcome them in. Let's see what they can do. This could be the start of a beautiful interplanetary partnership."

Ellie considered. In her heart of hearts, she was uneasy about the idea of running an event with those creatures standing in the middle of it. But what did Scripture say? Love thy neighbor. Judge not. Even the parts about entertaining angels unawares. And wasn't hospitality one of the core tenets of her faith? Care of the widow and the alien, she thought with a wry smile. And, in the end, there *was* the roof to consider.

"But—" Pastor Jonathan broke in.

"It's all right, Jon." Maybe she'd give the Gus method a try. "I think we'll go ahead with it."

Chapter Thirty-Three

The day of the fete was cool and gray, with storm clouds looming over the lake. Gus had found an old cane somewhere and was limping around the church grounds inspecting the preparations like a general getting ready to send his troops into battle. Even with the bad leg and the cane, he still somehow managed to project an air of strutting.

"That cutout's falling over," he said to the interns. "Anchor it down or something. We're gonna get a lot of wind here."

Todd and John Mark scurried off to fix the cardboard cutout of three little green men peering out of a flying saucer.

"Yes, yes," hissed Gus to himself. "Everything is proceeding as I have foreseen it."

The interns scurried back.

"Fill that dunk tank a little fuller. I wouldn't expect you to know this, but shallow dunk tanks are the leading cause of spine injury in the United States. I don't want that on my conscience."

"It said to fill it to the red line," said Simon uncertainly.

"Not on my watch," snapped Gus. "We want that water level kissing the dunk seat. Go. Go! What are you waiting for?"

"It's just, we'd have to get the hose back out and—"

"Fine. Forget it. They're going to be here any minute, anyway."

Gus limped over to his beach chair under the large tree, now located between a sausage stand and a beanbag toss game. He gingerly eased himself into it to survey his handiwork.

"WHAT ON EARTH? GUS!" shouted Pastor Ellie, charging across the grass from the parsonage. "I thought I told you to pull those down. People are going to start coming any minute now. What in the world are you thinking?"

"I think you mean, it's out of this world," said Gus smugly.

Ellie pointed at the giant banner hanging along the side of the church building.

"'All glory to our new alien overlords'? Seriously? You realize that's in incredibly poor taste."

"You know what my dad always said? Taste is what your neighbor ain't got."

"I'm serious, Gus. Take it down. What do you think people are going to think if they — how much did you spend on this? Did it ever occur to you that you could have just donated that to the fund instead of screwing around? Do you have any idea how hard we've been trying to—" She closed her eyes and took a deep breath. "You know what? Never mind. Not your problem. But that banner's about to be. Get it down. Now. And all the rest of this alien nonsense, too. It's entirely inappropriate. This is a church event, not a sci-fi convention. And people are already plenty nervous about—"

"Exactly! That's why I did it. Know thy enemy. That kind of thing. Demystify the Other a little, you know? You can't be scared when you're laughing. People will realize it's not such a big—"

"Do you see me laughing, Gus? I want that banner gone."

"It's not that simple! Those intern dudes are good with knots. Plus, with all the tarps up there, I think it's been subsumed. It's part of a whole rat king of cloth and ropes and banners. It is more machine now than man."

"I don't want to hear it. Just get it down."

Gus tried another tack. "Did you know you have very kind eyes? For a pastor, I mean."

"And pack up all these cardboard cutouts and nonsense. The Jorgensens are arriving. I'm going to go say hi to them. I want all this out of here. Now."

Pastor Ellie went off to greet the Jorgensens, her angry face replaced mid-stride with a cheery expression of welcome.

Gus settled back on his deck chair. "She'll come around. They all come around in the end."

BY NOON, the fete was in full swing, and Gus had been relegated to the role of carnival barker.

"Alien hunt," announced Gus half-heartedly. "Five dollars a throw. Save humanity. Be a big hero. Win the girl. Five dollars. Anybody for an alien hunt? Come on."

All his cardboard cutouts of aliens and flying saucers were clustered in the nook between two of the church's buttresses, overshadowed by the crumbling church wall. Ellie specifically ordered him to get them out of sight, but to Gus's mind, it was aesthetically displeasing and contrary to the spirit of a church fete to have a pile of abandoned cardboard cutouts sitting in a corner.

Instead, he'd decided to make lemons out of sour grapes. So he'd shanghaied a few of the beanbags from the beanbag toss and at his direction the interns wrangled a cutout or two into a new alien hunt game. Simon had timidly suggested reducing the price to fifty cents a throw, which to Gus's mind betrayed exactly the yokel-ish lack of vision that was going to lead to the town's inevitable downfall.

"Alien hunt," he repeated, with no one in earshot. "Double or nothing. Ten bucks a pop. Come on, people. Hunt it up."

Gus had to hand it to Pastor Ellie. She was a resourceful opponent. Over his strenuous objections, she had recruited Todd and John Mark to do her dirty work and deal with the banner. Turncoats.

As he'd predicted, the knots holding the banner up had proven impregnable, but with the strategic rearrangement of a few tarps to cover up some words here and there, the banner now read: ALL GLORY TO OUR LORDS.

They hadn't managed to cover up the S, and it seemed to Gus the final result was, if anything, more directly offensive to her target demographic, but that was hardly his concern. Indeed he relished the irony. *Sic semper tyrannosaurus* and all that.

Still, the whole event was taking a rather churchier turn than Gus would have preferred. Very provincial. He'd thought the alien hunt would be a fun little irony to pass the time until conditions were right for the Welcome Ceremony, but it was simply and irredeemably lame.

"Big chance to defeat the invaders. Alien hunt. Who wants to hunt some … annnnnd we're done here."

Perhaps Journey could be persuaded to wander the booths with him. The whole scene would be much improved by a little female company.

He let his sample beanbag drop to the ground then began limping away, leaving the alien hunt to operate on the honor system.

Chapter Thirty-Four

Aside from the fact that everybody involved knew it was a completely futile effort, the church fete looked like a fun outing. The church building was decorated with colorful bunting and balloons that took the edge off the ominous clouds gathering overhead. The grounds were set up with booths and games and food tents.

The knitting circle had a booth with handmade hats and scarves and sweaters and doilies for sale. The inevitable bake sale table was loaded down with an even greater abundance than usual of cookies and pound cake and lemon bars and chocolate chip bars and …well, all sorts of bars, really.

Somehow, someone had convinced Thor Halvorssen to be the dunk tank victim. He smiled grimly at all comers as if daring them to laugh at his old-fashioned full-body red and white candy-striped swimming costume. Nestor had volunteered, of course, but the planning committee's immediate consensus was that Thor was the real catch.

There were yard games and feats of strength, and in

one corner, Barty Olufsen himself was cheerfully tending the grill at a booth selling hot dogs and kielbasa and burgers and cheap fatty steaks courtesy of the Peculiar Steakhouse.

Sam regarded a face painting booth with some trepidation, wondering whether it would be a faux pas to refuse a face painting. Or, for that matter, to get one. It was hard to tell what constituted proper participation in these little local shindigs.

He felt an almost overpowering obligation to help as much as he could, to bring an infusion of his big-city software developer income into this small, well-meaning, downtrodden town that had seen a few lean years in a row. And that mainly seemed to mean buying a little something at practically every booth, whether he needed it or not.

He kind of wished he could write a check and be done with it, but there seemed to be something of a taboo against that. Or maybe he was just imagining it. That was the difficulty with local taboos. As the big city interloper, asking for clarification about them was roughly as taboo as the prohibited act itself. And besides, writing a check would have brought with it all of its own uncertainties about seeming cheap or showy or overly concerned with how he was coming across.

No. There were rules to it, customs as old as time. It was, in a way, like money laundering. Except instead of spreading illegitimate money around into legitimate businesses, it was about spreading charity through channels that made it acceptable, that absolved the breach of pride.

Better to simply make the rounds and buy too many funnel cakes and a scarf he was unlikely to wear and more lunch than he could possibly eat and, depending on how things went, possibly get his face painted. Maybe Spider-Man. Just to show he was willing to participate, of course.

It would have been much easier to spend the requisite money if he were buying for more than one. His mind turned to Journey, and then skipped away. That was dangerous territory.

Maybe another funnel cake.

Chapter Thirty-Five

Gus slipped his arm through Journey's.

"I said as *friends*," she snapped, and made to pull away.

But Gus spoke quickly to reassure her. "No, no. Just so I can guide you. You know. Make sure you don't bump into anything." She began to protest, but he held her off. "No. You're good. They've just got it set up all different than usual. I don't want you to trip or whatever."

"Fine," she said. Then, grudgingly. "Thanks."

Gus surveyed the surroundings. Yes. All was going well. A few glitches here and there, of course, but nothing insurmountable. The titans were behaving themselves. People were giving them a wide berth but for the most part seemed to have accepted them as part of the landscape. He had a beautiful woman on his arm. Funnel cake was in his near future.

He spotted Sam a couple booths away, wandering aimlessly with two plates of kielbasa.

"Hey, it's Sam."

"Really?" Journey asked eagerly. "Let's get him over here. Hey, Sam!"

"No. Yeah. I mean, it looks like he's kind of busy." Then, catching her face, he shrugged. "Then again, why not?"

"Sam! Over here!" she called again.

A happy thought occurred to Gus. "Actually, yeah. Get him over here. Hey, Sam!"

Sam looked up and a funny little grin split his face. He started walking over, his thin paper plates wobbling dangerously.

"Hey, guys." His eyes darted to their linked arms. "I didn't realize you were — I mean, that's great. It's great to see you. Both."

"Yeah," Gus said, glowing at Sam's assumption that he and Journey were together. "Just living the dream, you know?"

"Yeah. Totally. Me, too." Sam's plates wobbled again. "Hey, can we find somewhere to sit?"

"You got sausages?" Journey asked. "That smells amazing. I want one."

"Totally," Sam said. "Here, and actually—"

"What's that on your face?" asked Gus.

Sam instinctively tried to look down at his cheek. "What, this? Oh, that's not—"

"Is that Spider-Man?" asked Gus.

"No! I mean, yeah. I mean, technically—"

"You got your face painted? That's so dorky! Let me see." Journey leaned close to Sam and half-raised her hand.

"Don't touch it," Sam said.

"Of course not."

She leaned in closer, and for a second, Gus had the crazy thought that she might kiss him.

But she just gave a delicate sniff an inch or two from Sam's cheek. "Oh, my god. I wish I could see it. I want one!" She tugged on Gus's arm. "Which way to the face paints?"

"I've got an extra kielbasa if you want one," Sam offered.

Journey's face lit up, and once again Gus felt a pang of irritation.

"Here, let's find a table," Sam said.

"Aren't you listening? We're getting face paints, you dork." Gus chuckled and turned to Journey. "What a dork. Right?"

Journey grabbed Sam around the neck in an affectionate sort of pseudo-hug.

"Yeah, but he's our dork. I say we keep him."

"Watch out!" Sam cried as the kielbasas gave another dangerous wobble. "Actually, you know what? Never mind. You two are just … *here*." He thrust them at Gus. "I wanted to get a couple more of these anyway."

"No, stay," Journey cajoled.

"Really?" Sam asked.

"No, go," said Gus. "In fact, I'd love a funnel cake while you're at it."

Journey gave him a sharp look.

"What? I'm joking. Stay, stay." Gus made to grab Sam around the neck in a friendly tussle.

"No, don't!" One of Sam's damp paper plates finally succumbed, sendin g a sausage flopping to the grass amid a cascade of sauerkraut.

"I need to find somewhere to put these — this — down." Sam glanced at the fallen food like he was trying to figure out a way to clean up the lawn without spilling his other plate.

"That's fine," said Gus, sensing an opening. He looked around for a table. "Why don't you go do that. Or whatever. We'll rendezvous with you when we … you know.

Later. In a little bit. Soon," he amended quickly, trying to head off another protest from Journey. "I don't want him to spill all his stuff. Maybe next time don't buy three lunches. You're like a little kielbasa pig."

"Gus!" Journey snapped.

"Oh, it's not that," Sam said mildly. "I'm just trying to, you know. Support the thing. Or whatever. It's kind of hard to do in such small increments. But hey. More funnel cake for us, right?"

Journey smiled. "That's sweet."

"Should have come by the alien hunt," Gus muttered.

"I thought you were on their side," said Sam, confused.

"No, not — Look. This has been fun. Really great. But speaking of the titans, I've actually got somewhere to be. Somewhere important," Gus added, glancing at Journey to see if this got the right reaction. "Things to do, people to see. You know what I mean?"

"Not exactly," said Sam.

"Well, Journey knows what I'm talking about. Don't you?" Without waiting for a reply, he grabbed her hand then began leading her away from Sam toward the low stage at the center of the fete.

"What about Sam?" asked Journey with a touch of panic.

"Oh, he'll be fine here. He doesn't like getting in front of crowds. Stage fright. You know. Come here, big guy."

Sam rolled his eyes.

But the titan began walking toward them.

Ever since their arrival, they had seemed almost statuesque, first standing back to back, now spaced out a little and silently surveying the fete. They were in a different position than they'd been earlier, but this was the first time other than when they'd walked into town that he had actually seen one of them move.

It was slow and powerful and graceful, with an unearthly authority. At some semi-conscious level, it felt like the alien was the point of reference and it was simply moving its legs while waiting for its destination to arrive. It was little uncanny.

Sam wondered whether the handshake had somehow given Gus the power to control the aliens. Or just communicate with them, maybe. He supposed he didn't have to be able to control someone to get it to walk over toward you.

As the titan began moving, someone nearby shrieked. Then a ripple of fear spread through the crowd.

But Gus shouted, "Nothing to worry about. Nothing to worry about. Stay calm."

A voice in Sam's head was yelling at him to get up on the stage with them. But what could he do? Gus clearly had a plan. He was in obvious control of the situation. And Sam did hate getting in front of crowds.

Quick! He ordered himself. *Think of something!*

Which was not really helpful, in the final analysis. Sam was already thinking of something. Quite a few things. The look of outright fear on Journey's face. The titan slowly making its way to the stage as the crowd parted around it. Pastor Ellie vaguely yelling something from the dunk tank, where she'd taken her place after Thor's inevitable and glorious demise. Thinking of things didn't really do anything.

His hand itched for the hatchet he'd left back at Nestor's. Maybe if he had it he could — *what?* He grunted in disgust. What did he think he could do with a hatchet? Overthink it at the alien?

"Ladies and gentlemen," Gus said over the PA. "I am thrilled to welcome you to an event unprecedented in Lake Peculiar and, perhaps, in human history itself. Today we welcome guests from a galaxy far, far away!"

He emphasized this last line by shoving his face right up into the mic so it came out with a booming voice and a little reverb.

The crowd acted moderately impressed.

"I have communed with these beings, and I can vouch for them. They come in peace, and they seek to give us the secret to a brand-new age of enlightenment and prosperity."

A titan stepped onto the stage then stood just behind Gus and slightly to his right, an ominous presence over-shadowing them.

Journey clung to Gus's arm, looking pale and fright-ened and a little like she might throw up. She said some-thing to him, far too faintly for Sam to make out from this distance.

"Excuse me," Gus said, then he ducked away from the mic to consult with Journey.

Chapter Thirty-Six

Journey felt a thrill of fear as Gus began pulling her some-where, presumably up front for the welcoming ceremony.

"What about Sam?" she asked, knowing it wouldn't do any good. But she couldn't stand the thought of being up there alone with Gus. She could already feel the oppressive presence of the strangers looming behind her.

"Oh, he'll be fine," said Gus offhandedly and, she thought, maybe a little vindictively. "He doesn't like getting up in front of crowds. Stage fright. You know. Come here, big guy."

She wasn't sure what that last part meant at first. He'd said it with the sort of careless affection you might use toward a big dog. Then she felt one of the titans start moving.

Fear took hold.

Journey let herself be led through the crowd and up onto a low stage. Her whole attention was fixed on the thing she could feel moving closer and closer. It was slow, deliberate, powerful. There was too much crowd noise for her to distinguish the sound of its approach, but still, somehow, she knew exactly where it was, like a malevolent presence in her mind. Like someone glaring at the back of her head because she'd cut in front of them in line, but a hundred times stronger and infinitely cold, calm, calculating.

"Ladies and gentlemen!" boomed Gus into the microphone. Images flickered through her mind unbidden. Clattering insect-like legs. A pale planet. A gaping, unearthly hunger.

The oppressive weight of the stranger's presence felt like it might crush her. She tried to breathe. Tried to resist.

Gus was saying something, but she couldn't focus on it.

It felt like the stranger was trying to reach out, trying to invite her in, like some gentle brick that didn't know its slightest touch could crush her mind.

No! she screamed. *Leave me alone.*

Something shifted. The oppression was no lighter, but the stranger went away, like it had turned its attention to other things.

Journey took another labored breath. She could barely think, but a part of her knew this was her only chance. She had to act now or all would be lost. "Gus."

"Excuse me," boomed Gus's voice over the PA, then, off-mic, "What's wrong? What's going on?"

"Gus, we can't do this. We have to stop."

"No, no. It's fine. Trust me," he said in that greasy infuriating way he had.

She couldn't argue him down, especially not in her current state.

The stranger's presence dominated her thoughts. She wondered if it was pressing in on the others like it had been on her, if anyone else would figure out how to yell at it to go away. Or whether the others would even want to. For all she knew, they would be like Gus, eager to welcome the strangers in. Eager to receive their gifts, learn from them, sit at their feet. Start swaying.

No.

She took a moment to collect herself, told herself it had to be done. A small sacrifice, if this was all it took for her to save the town.

"Let's go somewhere else. And make out. Call off the welcome and let's get out of here. Together."

Gus took in a startled breath. Then she heard a slow smile dawning in his voice. "A kiss before the end of the world."

SAM STRAINED to hear what Gus was saying off mic, but it was impossible from his place in the crowd. He should be doing something. But what?

Nestor's words came back to him unbidden.

Your friend is going to do something you just can't stand by, and when you see that—

When I see it, what?

All he could see was the titan looming behind Gus while he and Journey had some kind of inaudible conversation. Gus looked confused, then eager. Journey was clearly in some sort of distress. She looked like she was struggling to speak.

Gus reached out and put a hand on her waist, started leaning in—

Simple enough. Don't just stand by.

"Wait!" Sam dashed toward the stage. "Excuse me," he said, trying to make his way past the people between him and the abomination on the stage. He glanced up to see Journey had laid a hand on Gus's chest to hold him back. But she hadn't turned away, or run off, or anything. The titan was standing paralyzed behind them, peering into the middle distance, the worst chaperone ever.

"Wait!" Sam shouted again, stepping up onto the low platform that served as a stage and grabbing the mic before Gus could react.

"Everyone, if you'll just listen to me for a second—"

Gus whirled to face him, and he took a few steps back, using the titan as a sort of human shield. Well, alien shield.

"I have to tell you something." Sam looked up at the titan and gulped.

It was at least seven feet tall and very powerful. This close to it, he could feel some weird flickering in his mind, like a radio scrolling through channels and failing to find a strong signal. A sort of headache or something. His mind jerked to Ronan's warnings, but he was done hiding. If the aliens hadn't figured out he was against them by now, maybe one big play was worth the risk.

"I'm afraid I have some bad news. I have reason to believe these entities are not acting in our best interest. I didn't say anything at first because — well, I had some reasons, but they were bad ones, I guess, or at least not good enough—"

He suddenly realized how many people were watching him, and what an awful job he was doing. His brain reset.

"Sorry. Let me try that again. Journey. I'm really sorry. For everything. I should have — *gah!* Why is this so complicated?"

"Give me that!" bellowed Gus, who thus far had seemed unwilling to make any sudden moves near the titan but was apparently conquering his reluctance.

"Gus, wait!" cried Journey, distracting him long enough for Sam to try again.

"What I'm trying to say is, these aliens might be dangerous, and we shouldn't trust them. Necessarily. Yet. Maybe later, but we have to be sure before we, you know, welcome them in and accept whatever they're giving us and all that."

Gus grabbed the mic. "That's what I was going to say!"

"It was?" cried Sam, confused. "I thought you were going to do a welcome ceremony and all that. Dawn of the new age, et cetera."

"Dude, shut up," hissed Gus off mic. "You're totally anti-wingmanning me here."

"What do you mean? That's not even a thing."

"I'm afraid something's come up," announced Gus over the PA, "and the welcome ceremony is canceled."

"He already said that!" shouted someone from the crowd.

"He's right," said Journey, sounding like someone who was feeling both great relief and a terrible headache. "Sam already saved the day."

"I did?"

"He did?"

"Deal's off, " said Journey. "Here, let me have the mic for a minute."

"No way!" Gus yanked it away. She was still couple paces away and not making any obvious move for the microphone. And blind. Gus raised the mic to his lips. "Sorry. Cancel that. It's back on. Dawn of a new age, everyone. Come forward and receive the gift of the titan!"

Sam looked up at the alien and tried to weigh his chances. The thing looked like it could smash him to jelly if it decided to. Of course, he'd never seen them make a sudden move. Other than leveling Moscow.

A distant rumble of thunder rolled across the lake.

With a nervous sound, he steeled himself, then began shouting into the crowd.

"Don't listen to Gus! He's … he's …" He raged against

the part of him that couldn't make the words come out. What was he even scared of? Gus was an idiot. It wasn't like he could actually beat Sam up or anything. Still, the words wouldn't come. "I mean. I've known him a long time. And you don't really want to listen to everything he—"

"Step right up," said Gus with grand confidence. And a microphone. "Enlightenment and blessings await you. These visitors from the heavens are ready to welcome us into their bosom." He glanced to the edge of the stage, where one of the interns was watching everything unfold with faint amazement. "That's a thing, right? Like, a religious thing?"

"Yeah. Sure," said the intern. "Bosom of Abraham and all that."

"Into their bosom!" Gus resumed with vigor.

"No!" shouted Journey desperately.

Sam kept trying to shout over Gus, but it was a losing battle. It probably would have been one if Sam had a microphone and Gus didn't, much less the other way around.

Still. He had to try.

"I'll just say Gus got us in some bad trouble on a few different occasions, even just on our way up here. He made me duct tape spikes to the front of our car then they fell off and tore the tires to shreds and we would've been totally stranded if Ronan hadn't—"

"Listen to the man," cried Gus into the mic. "This charlatan would have you believe I quote-unquote 'forced' him to tape spikes to the front of a car. Who would force such a thing? Who could? And is he not, in complying, the true—"

"Here," said the intern, suddenly appearing by Sam side with the second mic.

"Oh, awesome. Thanks!" Sam flipped it on then resumed his attempts to say anything bad about Gus. "I'm just saying he's not the smartest, you know … tool … in the drawer. Or shed, or whatever. You might not want to trust whatever he's trying to sell you."

Gus continued to bluster. "I speak to you as one who has communed with the titans. They showed me great and wondrous things, the likes of which mankind has not known."

A sprinkle of rain started, and Sam felt a surge of hope. Maybe if he could just hold things off until the rain kicked in, that might at least buy them some time.

"Line up! Receive the gift of the titan. Here. I'll show you. It's perfectly safe."

"No!" shouted Sam and Journey in unison.

But Gus had already turned his back to the crowd, his face tipped up toward the titan with his eyes closed and a faint smile of spiritual bliss, awaiting the gift.

"Everyone listen to me," cried Sam, no longer thinking about his words. "Gus is an idiot. This isn't safe."

"You're an idiot!" snapped Gus, turning back momentarily to glare at Sam.

That was it, Sam realized. Gus had to have the last word. That was the strategy.

"Well, you're the one who thought Journey was supposed to be your girlfriend. That's the whole reason you dragged us out here in the first place. A kiss before the end of the world. How's that going for you?"

Gus had faced the titan again, but this pulled him back. "Shut up! What the hell do you know about it? You've never even kissed a girl in your life. Not like me. I've kissed plenty of girls."

"I've kissed three different girls!" countered Sam.

"Randi Patella in third grade, Darcy Belafonte in ninth grade, and that girl — you know. With the thing?"

"She doesn't count!" snapped Gus.

"Fine. How many girlfriends have you had? *Not* counting in a video game."

"I'm not so crass that I consider that a primary measure of my success in life!"

Classic Gus move. Win when when he could win, high road you when he couldn't.

"Yeah, well if she wasn't your *barely, technically*" — Sam pinched his fingers a micron apart — "*just* under the wire girlfriend, I'd already have asked her out myself! Sorry if that's weird," he added, turning to Journey, though with his current momentum, it came out more angry than apologetic.

"Oh, please. You think you're this big man," mocked Gus. "Going around all careful and whatever, like you think you know what you're doing. Like it wasn't you that put those spikes on the car and got us stranded. Like it wasn't you that blew our cover with Ronan. You wouldn't even have left the house if it weren't for me. You'd be getting picked over by an angry mob. Hell, you wouldn't have left Williamsburg. You'd probably be flipping burgers at some two bit hot dog stand right now if I hadn't called you out on the great adventure."

"Great adventure! What the hell kind of a great adventure is that? Living in middle of Nowhere, Iowa, working at some dead end data job? Polo shirt and khakis every day? Highlight of the week is when the new comic books come out? You call that an adventure? This is an adventure! We're finally actually doing something. We finally actually matter. And you're about to lead the whole town into a pit just because you're so desperate for your one goddamn moment in the spotlight!"

"I'm not desperate for anything. I'm trying to lead these people into enlightenment and a new age. You think there's ever been a chance like this before, *ever in history?* You think we're gonna get a prize for taking it slow and dotting our T's and crossing our I's? This is our chance to put Lake Peculiar on the map. This is our chance to be heroes. Make a name for ourselves for once in our lives. You don't think the titans are offering the same gift to a thousand little crowds all across the country this very minute? And eight hundred of them are gonna pick up pitchforks and torches and all but five of the rest are going to go into committee about it and talk themselves to death until the titans get sick of it and flatten the town or move on or whatever they're gonna do, and those last five or ten are going to rise to greatness, except one of them will do it first. And I don't know about you, but I don't want us to be number four and I sure as hell don't want us to kill this thing in goddamn committee!"

"And what if you're wrong? Damn it, Gus. Get past your assumptions and your self-centered whatever for just one second and *think*. Have you ever been right one single time this entire trip? Or ever? You keep jumping us off cliffs and forcing me to figure out how to fly on our way down. You're only here because I have saved your butt so many times, and you don't even notice I'm doing it."

"My butt? *My* butt? What about your butt? You're like the most nervous little nothing of a person I've ever met! Geez." Gus addressed the crowd. "You try to do a guy a favor, and this is what you get? Are you really going to listen to what Scaredy McGee over here has to say? Or are we going to do this thing while we still have some chance at greatness? Who's with me?"

"Please," Sam begged the crowd. "Don't listen to him. He doesn't know what he's talking about. We don't know anything about these creatures. You really want to just let them into your mind? Let them do who knows what with our town?" It struck him only after he'd said it that he had called Lake Peculiar *our town*. He tucked that away for later. "How do we know we can trust them? How do we even know what they're allegedly offering us?"

"I told you," snapped Gus. "I talked to them. I mean, not talked, but you know. Communed. Or whatever. Their intentions are good. Look at me. I'm fine. I'm better than ever. And that was just from handshakes. I'm like a whole different — you know."

"Exactly! And that doesn't worry you?"

"I don't know, Sam. I guess this is where we decide whether we're going to live by our worries or rise above them." His eyes darted to Journey. "You know, I really tried with you. But I'm done. I guess nothing is enough. So go kiss whatever you want. I don't need you anymore."

He turned back to the titan.

"A kiss before the dawn of the world," he said, and dropped the mic.

"No! Gus. Please. I'm sorry. You don't have to—"

But Gus wasn't listening anymore. Not to Sam or anyone else. His face was turned up, his eyes closed, and the rain was beginning to fall.

The titan grasped his head, a huge powder-white hand below each jaw.

The better to snap your neck, deary, said some parody of the Big Bad Wolf in Sam's head.

In Sam's mind, the hands pressed harder and harder until they crushed Gus's head like a grape.

One sudden twist, lifting his head high above the crowd as his body collapsed onto the stage.

They grabbed the hair and began pulling, pulling, until—

But none of that happened.

The titan bent low and touched its lips to Gus's forehead. Not exactly a kiss, not the way humans would do it. More like the action of something that had ransacked human minds to find a gesture they considered significant, then performed a reasonably accurate imitation.

Gus's eyes flickered closed. The rain picked up. His knees sagged.

"Gus!" Sam cried. He felt a wave of psionic energy wash through his mind. Images skittered through his head — a field of stars, a pale white world, and others too fleeting to capture, too bizarre to comprehend.

Journey cried out in pain and fell to her knees on the stage, clutching her forehead. A gasp and a murmur rolled through the crowd.

An untouchable moment passed. The hush of rain carried across the lake's surface.

The titan resumed its statuesque pose.

Sam swallowed. More images flicked through his mind. Gus grinning in victory before he collapsed. Gus's head falling off, followed immediately by his arms and legs. Gus spontaneously bursting into flame.

Gus's eyes opened. He turned to the crowd, lifted his arms in triumph. "We will be magnificent!" he bellowed. And he didn't need a microphone for every ear to hear him. The crowd broke out in spontaneous applause. "Who will join us?"

There was a crack of thunder, then the storm began. What had been a light rain under looming clouds moments ago suddenly broke into torrential buckets pouring from the sky.

A general hubbub of shouting and shrieks arose from the crowd as people dashed around, everyone trying to grab whatever needed to come in out of the rain and get to the church or back to their cars in a mad frenzy.

Gus watched, laughing with childlike delight, completely unconcerned that he was getting soaked to the bone.

Behind him, the titan began walking back toward the church, huge and inscrutable.

Sam was already soaked through in the time it took him to walk the three steps to where Journey knelt on the stage, rocking and moaning faintly. She looked up at him with a harrowed expression, her blind eyes somehow peering directly into his. "We lost. It's too late. They got him."

"No." He helped her to her feet. "We held him off. We kept them from getting the rest of the town. For now, at least." Sam began leading her back to the parsonage. "Now, let's get inside."

They scurried through the rain, dashing across a lawn already turning marshy. He dodged and wove through the frenzy of people bringing in whatever decorations and equipment they could salvage. Journey gripped tight to his arm and ran beside him, like he'd never imagined a blind girl could, as a catharsis of sobbing and laughter poured from her body. They dashed up onto the porch and, finally sheltered, came to a stop, breathless, as a wall of rain crashed to earth around them.

Journey was still holding his arm, and now she leaned against it. He slipped it around her waist, and it occurred to him that he had put his arm around her without a second thought, as if it was the most natural thing in the world.

He rarely did anything without a third thought, at minimum.

Sam smiled.

Maybe there was something to this new strategy of *not* overthinking everything. He'd have to give it a try.

She turned to face him, and her face was serious and beautiful.

"Did you mean what you said? About asking me out?"

Sam swallowed. But for once, he didn't feel hesitant or uncertain. "Totally. One hundred percent. Look, I know it's not really exactly right, with you and Gus and everything, but yeah. That's what I want. If you're ever up for it."

"What do you mean, me and Gus?" she asked, seeming genuinely confused. "That's the second time you said that."

"You know. Since he's your boyfriend and everything. I know you guys are on a little bit of a break or whatever. IRL. Until you get to, you know. And normally I wouldn't … I mean. There's a code and all that. But I think I would have been willing to take a pass just this once. I mean. If you were into it, obviously. And if you and Gus weren't already … I'm not trying to … you know."

"He's not my boyfriend."

"What?"

"Why did you even think he was?"

His mind reeled. It was like asking why you thought it was dark at night. There wasn't really a why to how things were. "You're Night Fox, right? And I saw you two together. At the fete."

She wrinkled her nose and scoffed. "I was just trying to stay close enough to screw up his plans. After you … well, anyway. I thought I might have to act on my own. So I stuck as close as I could. But I only let him take me there as friends. God. Me and Gus?" She let out a long and incredulous laugh.

"But you're Night Fox!" Sam said again.

"What the hell is Night Fox?"

"I thought you two were, you know. Like, an item. In the game."

"What game?

"Warduster?" Something wasn't connecting, and Sam was growing uneasy.

"Never heard of it."

"What? We play all the time. You called Gus to pick you up in your in-game messaging. We've been—"

Journey's eyes widened. "Oh, my God."

"What?"

"I'm gonna kill her." Journey started laughing.

"What? Kill who?"

"She must've done it. Grandma June. She's a hard-core gamer from way back. I never really got into it much.

"Wait, you're saying Night Fox — like, *the* Night Fox, Gus's online Canadian girlfriend Night Fox — is your *grandma?*"

"Looks like it."

"But why didn't she say anything?"

"Oh, I don't know. It's not exactly the most comforting thing to tell a blind girl about to get kicked out of her home. 'Hey, honey. I thought of some guys who might be able to help us. I met them on this dumb game I play online. Should be fine.'"

Sam was about to protest that Warduster wasn't dumb, but Journey laughed, and he suddenly didn't care about his dumb game at all.

Journey turned her face toward his. For a long moment, she peered at him so hard, he almost forgot she couldn't see him.

"You thought all that, and you still stood up to him?"

"Yeah. I mean, I guess. Yeah."

"You know they're still going to listen to him."

"Yeah. Probably. But at least we bought ourselves some time."

She smiled, a sad, hopeful little smile. "A kiss before the end of the world?"

Sam didn't think twice.

Chapter Thirty-Seven

The sun was high by the time Sam woke the next morning. He and Journey had been up talking and strategizing most of the night, and by the end, he'd caught a couple hours of sleep on the couch in the parsonage basement.

He ran a hand along the kitchen table, feeling good. He would find Ronan and get his ideas on how to best convince the town to reject the aliens. Journey had been dreading going to sleep more than ever now that she knew the dream was true, but Sam had pointed out that it was an excellent chance to watch for clues. Free intel, really.

And he would have a good talking-to with Gus. Figure out the gaps in his story. Gus could put up a good enough front for a little while, but in the end he was all bluster. After all their years as friends, Sam would be able to cut through his bullshit, no problem. Up until now, he'd had trouble calling Gus on it, but he had a feeling that wouldn't be as much of a problem anymore.

And really, who had any reason to say the aliens had anything to offer? It was a temporary high at best, some kind a mind game that made people feel good. With any luck, it wore off overnight. There was a decent chance Gus had a horrible hangover or something right now.

Sam stepped onto the porch and his jaw dropped.

The church building was different. The aliens had changed position. One was kneeling in front of the front steps. One was kneeling on the lawn between him and the church. He couldn't see the third, but it was probably on the other side.

In between them, the church building was resplendent, shot through and built up with some kind of blue crystalline substance. The roof was fused with azure crystal, its historic decorations restored and enhanced with an alien extrapolation of the soaring patterns. The new shimmering blue roof was supported by buttresses, curves of glassy blue soaring out into empty air, then plunging thick beautiful columns into the earth. The steeple was now at the core of a branching spire yawning toward the sky.

It was magnificent.

It was impossible.

It was miraculous.

Journey stepped out onto the porch of the parsonage beside him.

"Hey," he said.

"Beautiful day," she remarked.

Sam's heart settled into the pit of his stomach. So much for convincing the town the aliens had nothing to offer.

And if there had been any doubt that Journey's dreams were accurate, that was gone.

It was starting. The pale bald strangers. The crystal blue church. The swaying cultists.

And there was no telling what price they would pay to stop it.

He took Journey by the waist, still staring up at the miraculous sapphire cathedral.

He swallowed.

"Totally."

The Invasion of Lake Peculiar continues...

Sam may have stopped Lake Peculiar from being sucked into the alien hive mind, but he hasn't convinced Gus, or the rest of the town, that aliens aren't the best thing since fried cheese curd balls.

Can Sam break out of his co-dependent loyalty to Gus to lead a resistance against the aliens and their mind-altering "gifts"?

Pick up Fun with Mind Control today

A Quick Favor

If you enjoyed this book, would you please take a moment to write a short review on your favorite online bookstore so other readers can enjoy it, too?

Thanks so much!
    Jack Ravenhill

About the Author

Jack Ravenhill loves to build strange and complex worlds rich with unforgettable characters, hidden corners, and looming questions. His favorite stories break down old categories and invite you into fresh and fascinating ways of thinking. Whether it's robot fairies or small-town aliens, whether the stakes are the fate of the world or a teenage heartbreak, Jack always gets you through with heart, humor, and a feast among friends.

Lightning Source UK Ltd.
Milton Keynes UK
UKHW010844070223
416609UK00003B/997